Peter Moir Fotheringham was born in the Bridge of Allan, in Central Scotland, and still lives in the area. He left school at seventeen to be a newspaper reporter, then went into land survey. He took early retirement to concentrate on his writing. He has had nine books published, including his previous novel *Death of a Fading Beauty*, and has sold about two hundred short stories as well as comedy material for radio and television.

THE MAN WHO BLEW HIS MIND

Michael Bannerman could remember just a few months of his life, and during most of that time he had been locked in a small room at the Institute. For the past two months he had been in the community, trying to recover his mind. He was the victim of a traffic accident, he had been told. But the regular nightmares suggested a different story, a story of violence in an African country gripped by civil war. Only as his memory returned did he begin to understand the enormity of what he had done and why he was so important — and he was determined never to reveal the secrets locked in his mind, no matter what they did to him.

Books by Peter Moir Fotheringham
Published by The House of Ulverscroft:

THE MILLENNIUM TRAIL
SEASNAKE
DEATH OF A FADING BEAUTY
DEATH OF A LONELY WARRIOR

PETER MOIR FOTHERINGHAM

◆

THE MAN WHO BLEW HIS MIND

Complete and Unabridged

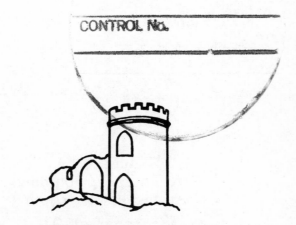

ULVERSCROFT
Leicester

First published in Great Britain in 2001 by
Robert Hale Limited
London

First Large Print Edition
published 2003
by arrangement with
Robert Hale Limited
London

British Library CIP Data

Fotheringham, Peter Moir
The man who blew his mind.—Large print ed.—
Ulverscroft large print series: adventure & suspense
1. Amnesia—Fiction
2. Suspense fiction 3. Large type books
I. Title
823.9′14 [F]

ISBN 0–7089–4787–5

Published by
F. A. Thorpe (Publishing)
Anstey, Leicestershire

Set by Words & Graphics Ltd.
Anstey, Leicestershire
Printed and bound in Great Britain by
T. J. International Ltd., Padstow, Cornwall

This book is printed on acid-free paper

1

'Stratton Fields Garage. Mary speaking. How may I help you?'

He listened to her singsong voice and checked his name on the envelope pinned to the wall beside the phone.

'My name's Michael Bannerman. I put my car in for a service this morning. Nissan Sunny.' He quoted the registration number. 'Is it ready?'

'One moment, please.'

He listened to the music and stared at the envelope and silently repeated his name several times. It was odd how he could rattle off the registration number of the car but had so much difficulty with his own name. Sometimes it came easily, other times there was just an embarrassing blank. He always carried another envelope in his jacket pocket in case he needed it.

'Mr Bannerman? Your car will be ready in about half an hour. No problems.'

'Thank you. 'Bye.'

It was a ten-minute walk to the garage but he had shopping to do and if he did that on the way then he wouldn't have to look for a parking slot on the way back. At the flat door he stopped and went through the ritual: wallet, keys, envelope with his name on it, loose change, flick knife, cosh. Cleared to go.

He went downstairs. The Cartwrights from 1a were just getting home from walking their fat spaniel round the park, all three of them out of breath.

'You should have a coat, Mr Bannerman. It's parky out there.'

'I like it fresh, Mrs Cartwright. It's a pleasure.'

'He's a young man, Ella. He doesn't feel the cold like we do.'

He wondered how old he was. No one knew. Somewhere between thirty-five and forty, probably.

He did his shopping at the row of shops opposite the park. A crusty wholemeal and two danish from the baker, two steak mince pies from the butcher, a *Telegraph* from the newsagent. While he waited for his change he asked: 'Have you a copy of *Land Rover Owner International?*'

The shopkeeper scanned the shelves. 'Should be one, sir. Yes, here we go.'

Bannerman took the magazine and stared at it, puzzled.

* * *

2

Elliot Pryce had a problem with enclosed spaces. Not exactly claustrophobia, he insisted to himself, but edging that way. The basement at the Institute was one of his least favourite places, one he avoided unless there was a compelling reason for his being there. But Spire Matte Interco was a demanding and unforgiving company, a company where top management were expected to be available to work three hundred and sixty five days a year if required; it was not a company where one revealed personal weaknesses.

He followed Dr Grace down the concrete stairs, gripping the iron banister tightly, trying to hide the mounting tension.

'What's the latest on Bannerman?'

Angela Grace knew better than to refer the bastard Pryce to the reports she and Dr Leigh submitted every week; it would be a mistake to suggest that he hadn't read them. Elliot Pryce had clout and the people on his back had even more clout. Collectively, they had the power to close the Institute and dismiss everyone working there at a moment's notice. They had done so with other units of the company when the costs outweighed the potential. And Pryce was overbearing and aggressive, a shouter; the least said to him the better.

She paused at the basement door and gave

him an empty smile, hating his thin face and colourless eyes and the rat-trap mouth. Dr Angela Grace was not responsive to male charms, but Elliot Pryce was particularly repugnant. It was impossible to imagine any woman going willingly to bed with him.

'Success, Mr Pryce. He's been in the community for two months now and he has adapted very well indeed, considering what happened to him.' She had been with Spire Matte Interco long enough to know how dangerous it was to hint at anything less than total success.

'We'll see.' The remark carried an undercurrent of threat; so much of what Elliot Pryce said was threatening. She pushed open the door and held it for him and he entered the cramped room with no word of thanks. *I bet he learned that at business school*, she thought; *there was probably a course credit for Establishing Your Superiority.*

A dozen computer screens glowed in the semi-darkness. Two observers relaxed in wheeled swivel chairs, one of them wearing earphones. There was a strong smell of tobacco and coffee.

'This is John Valance and Martin Brown, the on-duty observers. This is Mr Pryce, from the Executive.'

Pryce ignored them and concentrated on

the screens, keeping his hands in his pockets to hide the nervous tremor. The gloom seemed to make the room even smaller, even more constrictive.

'What am I seeing?'

Dr Grace pointed. 'These two screens show Bannerman's sitting room; these two show his bedroom; this is his bathroom; this is his kitchen. This is the view from the tail car.'

'I don't see Bannerman. Where is he?'

'In the newsagent's. Letitia's with him.' Valance pointed to a screen. 'Here he comes.'

They watched Bannerman leave the shop and turn right and walk along the pavement, a plastic shopper in one hand. A black woman followed. They saw her hand cover her mouth.

'He bought a *Telegraph* and a copy of *Land Rover Owner International*.' The sound quality was very good. The picture jerked as the car moved off in pursuit.

Martin Brown held up a pad. 'He's also bought a loaf of bread, two danish pastries and two meat pies. That's about average, but the magazine is new. He's never done that before.'

'Never done what?' Pryce demanded. 'Bought a magazine?'

'He's bought a couple of computer magazines but never anything to do with

Land Rovers or cars or anything else. Sir.'

Pryce looked at Dr Grace. 'What's the significance of this?'

'I don't know. It's only just happened and . . . '

'Bloody find out!'

★ ★ ★

Bannerman collected the car and drove back to the flat and parked under the trees; he made coffee then sat at the table and stared at the magazine.

Why *Land Rover Owner International*?

He went through it page by page. Land Rover conversions, Land Rover events, Land Rovers crossing a desert, rebuilding a Series I ragtop, replacement engines, soundproofing, tyres, shock absorbers, readers' letters, Land Rovers for sale.

It was another world. Clearly, he had no interest in Land Rovers. Until he asked for it he hadn't even known there was such a publication as *Land Rover Owner International*.

No clues. Nothing to open a window into his mind.

Ten minutes to four on a Thursday afternoon in a second floor flat in a quiet part of north London.

He stood at the window overlooking the back gardens and watched one man cutting his grass and another tying plants to sticks. Sweet peas, by the look of it. He could recognize sweet peas but he kept forgetting his own name.

He never left the flat without the knife and the cosh but he didn't know why he needed to protect himself or against whom and he asked for magazines he didn't know existed.

And maybe once every couple of weeks there was the nightmare. He would wake electrified with rage, his mind wild with images of gunfire and blood and terrified faces, fire and explosions, screaming, shouting, roaring engines, the stink of exhaust fumes and clouds of dust, rage and more rage.

But not fear; never fear. Which seemed odd. Fear would have been understandable, given the rest of the nightmare.

★ ★ ★

Elliot Pryce tried to relax in the swivel chair while he watched the screens showing Michael Bannerman drinking coffee and reading the magazine with stultifying thoroughness. He would have to report to the Executive at ten o'clock the following

7

morning and they would ask questions and it was imperative that he had all the answers. Just one woolly response, one moment of indecision, could ruin a man's career with SMI. It was an unforgiving environment.

'Is this normal? Is this what he does all day?'

Dr Grace had been anticipating the question. 'He reads a lot, spends a lot of time in the flat, a lot of time thinking. This particular magazine is new. He owned a Land Rover while he was in Africa, so I suppose that might be relevant. This may be important: it may be a memory, a connection. What we're desperately lacking is feedback. We need to know his reactions; we need to know what he's thinking and, of course, all we're getting is whatever he e-mails us every night, and he's not always as explicit as we'd like. What he needs is someone to talk to, someone to draw him out, so we can listen to him, but he hasn't made any friends or invited anyone back to the flat, which is what we'd hoped for.'

Which was exactly what she and Dr Leigh had been saying in their reports for the past four weeks.

'Well, for God's sake, arrange that. Find him a friend. Do it now.'

'Yes, sir.'

* * *

I need exercise, Bannerman thought, squeezing his thighs. I've been out of the flat just twice since the car was serviced and all I've done is drive to the library and back again via the shops. At the very least a walk round the park. Maybe I should do some sit-ups.

He went to the window; the sky was grey and the slates wet but the rain had stopped. Everything looked fresh and cool.

I used to long for days like this when . . .

He shook his head impatiently. *When* was a place and time hidden in the darkness behind his eyes. He'd make a note later and tell Dr Grace and Dr Leigh. Restless, he pulled on his raincoat and went to the door, checking his pockets as he went.

On the landing he met a plump young woman with a red face, a bulging holdall hanging by a strap from one shoulder and a cardboard box under her arm. He stood aside to let her pass and she made an exaggerated expression to indicate exhaustion.

'We should have taken a ground floor flat.'

'Can I help?'

'Would you, love? It'll save you having to resuscitate me.' She offered the cardboard box and he took it. Books, probably, judging by the weight. She was a big girl, tall and

9

heavily built, reddish-blonde hair untidy, clear-skinned, the blue eyes good-humoured. 'Thanks. I'm Liz, your new neighbour. Flat 3b. The small person staggering along at the back muttering words a young lady ought not to know is Marianne.'

'I'll carry your bag as well,' Bannerman said, glancing down the stairs at the top of a dark head. 'Michael. 2a. This door here.'

They had unloaded a taxi on to the pavement. It took three trips to carry everything upstairs and distribute their belongings between the two small bedrooms and the sitting room. Marianne was slim and slightly sallow, half her face hidden by unflattering glasses and too much dark hair.

'I need liquid,' Liz said, slumping into an armchair, her face flushed.

'I have cider in the fridge.' Bannerman said. 'Would that do?'

She grinned at him. 'We've found a knight in shining armour, Marianne. A man prepared to sweat on our behalf and then provide cold cider.'

'That would be lovely, Michael,' Marianne said. 'We'll repay the gesture when we're settled in.'

Her smile was an unexpected light in her face.

★ ★ ★

They knocked at his door on the Sunday and asked if he could recommend a good pub for lunch and invited him to join them. They were relaxed and funny and they all had a mutual interest in the *Sunday Times* crossword. They managed to finish it collectively, but only by making unjustified assumptions about the last two clues. Then they talked for a time, the women slightly drunk; they were both hospital sisters, old friends from the days when they started nursing, neither of them married, recently promoted and now working at a nearby hospital. When they got back to the flats he invited them in for coffee and an Eddie Izzard video.

★　★　★

When Bannerman went to the bathroom Liz looked up the cornice at one corner of the sitting room.

'Get all that? Call my mobile.'

The phone buzzed immediately and she heard the voice of John Valance, one of the technicians at the Institute.

'Got it. Dr Leigh wants to talk to you.'

'He'll have to be quick.'

'Hello, Liz. Well done. I've never seen him so relaxed and talkative. Push the matter of his past life any chance you get. It's clear he's more interested in Marianne than in you, so could you tell her to follow up, please. Tell her to get close to him.'

'OK.' Liz closed the connection and looked at Marianne. 'You've to get your knickers off, you lucky cow.'

★ ★ ★

Bannerman was watching the news on television on the Monday evening when the knock came at the door.

'Hello, Michael.'

'Hello, Marianne.'

'I made lasagne for Liz and myself then remembered she's meeting someone and I thought . . . '

'Come in.'

She was carrying a tray covered with a tea towel. She wore a freshly-ironed denim shirt and a short denim skirt and her straight dark hair looked as if it had been shampooed and brushed within the past half hour. She had a good figure and fine skin but she would never be beautiful. Pretty, perhaps, but it would require a serious change to her hairstyle and probably new glasses.

'I've made a salad as well.'

'Sounds good. Thank you. I had the choice

of a cheese sandwich or going out for a fish supper.' He opened a bottle of wine and they ate and the food was excellent.

'So how are things at work, Marianne? Have you sorted out your ward manager?'

'It's easy for you to say stand up to her, Michael, but when it comes to the bit . . . '

She was intelligent without being intellectual and, when the wine had relaxed her, quite witty. She was easy to talk to and she and her friend were the only human beings he had spent time with on a personal level since . . . since whenever. It was good to be with her.

They watched television for a while because he didn't know what else to suggest and she gradually slid along the couch until they were touching and he could feel her warmth through his shirt and smell her perfume. She had tucked up her legs on the seat and he could see her knees and most of her thighs and it was difficult not to stare. Something on the screen made them laugh and in that moment of sharing she raised his arm and put it round her narrow shoulders and wriggled closer, holding his hand. He could see down the front of her shirt to the sweet white curves of her cleavage.

Sex, it's called. Men and women together.

13

I know about it. It's been on the television often enough and I know I must have done it but I can't remember anything except that it's good and probably has something to do with the feeling I'm getting in my pants and the problem I often have first thing in the morning. Except that it's not really a problem.

He did nothing for several minutes then touched her chin and she raised her face and smiled and put a hand round the back of his neck and pulled him into a kiss. Soft mouth, warm and eager. He stroked her neck and she sighed and they kissed again and after a while, because he couldn't resist the urge, he drew his fingertips down her neck to her chest and she undid the buttons of her shirt. A small white bra, lacy round the top. He traced his fingers across the smooth flesh, amazed that this was happening, amazed that she was not resisting.

He knew what to do and why he was doing it but he had no recollection of ever having done it before.

He stopped, uncertain, and after a time she took his hand and placed it on her breast. He caressed the silky material then she murmured something he didn't catch and they kissed again.

'Bed?' he whispered.

'Yes.'

She undressed quickly, her back to him, and slid under the sheets. Narrow back, a pleasing stern, shapely legs. The very last thing she did was to take off her glasses and fold them neatly and put them on the bedside cabinet. He stripped and got in beside her, his eagerness all too evident, and switched off the light and the darkness seemed to release her from her inhibitions. It was as if she wanted to do everything at once. 'Kiss me here, Mike.' She cupped her breast and offered it to his mouth and pressed his head against her chest; when he moved his hand down she spread her legs, her body arching, making wordless sounds. When he tried to enter her she stopped him and from somewhere produced a condom and rolled it on.

'It would be good, but we can't risk any little accidents, Mike.'

She lay back and spread her legs and pulled him on top of her and they clung desperately to each other with no control over the swift climax.

Later, as he caressed her, she slid a thigh between his and teased his nipple with her mouth.

'So now I know how to get you into bed, Mike. Lasagne and salad. My God, what will

15

steak and chips do?'

'Is this really our first time?'

'What do you mean? Of course it's our first time.'

The scrambled images must have been of some other woman. Or women. 'We made love like we'd done it before.'

'Maybe you'd been planning it, Mike. I had. Lying in my bed upstairs, thinking about you, getting all hot and bothered. I knew we'd do it eventually, when you got over your shyness. I just got impatient, waiting for you to make the first move. I sent out enough signals but you didn't seem to be receiving them. You shouldn't be so shy.'

'Can't help it.'

She giggled and moved her hand down his stomach. 'You're not all shy.'

He could remember how long he'd known her but not that they hadn't made love. She had been living upstairs, sharing with the other girl, for a week or so. The other girl was . . . Liz. They were both nurses.

'I know hardly anything about you, Mike. Is that bad of me? Sleeping with you when I know hardly anything about you?'

'You've known me for a while.'

'Yes, but you haven't said much about yourself. What's this?'

She had found the long scar on the inside of his left thigh.

'I was in a car accident.'

'I felt something up here as well. Yes, here.' Her fingers stroked his right side just below the ribs. 'Same accident?'

'Yes. It was quite messy.'

'Poor you. Is that when you broke your nose and split your eyebrow?'

'Yes.' That's what they'd told him. He had no memory of it.

Her hand went back down the bed and she giggled again. 'I'm glad nothing important was damaged. Everything seems to be in fine working order.'

For a plain and diffident young woman she was surprisingly forward in bed. Later, when they made love again, it was with her on top, noisy and uninhibited.

'Sexual frustration, three glasses of wine and a sexy man,' she said afterwards, catching her breath. 'It's a potent mixture.'

'Am I sexy? Or were you just seriously frustrated?'

'You're sexy. Liz and I could never work out why you didn't have a woman, why you never came on to us. We gave you plenty of chances. We even thought you might be gay, except there weren't any men either. Just that middle-aged couple who visited.'

'Family.' Dr Grace and Dr Leigh, on their weekly visit.

'I don't even know what you do for a living, Mike. I remember asking, but you were vague. Something about writing.'

'I'm working on a book.'

'What about?'

'Guilt and introspection and doubt.'

He could clearly remember the afternoon at the Institute when they put together that particular part of his fake background. It had been almost like a parlour game, everyone trying to be funnier than everyone else. An in-depth study of codpieces; an examination of the influence of Dylan Thomas on pre-civil war American railroad expansion; a murder mystery involving a monopedes' basketball team; Iceland, the new St Tropez; a gay western called A Fistful of Dollies with an erotic sequel called. For A Few Dollies More. The final decision was that a serious mainstream novel was likely to create fewer awkward questions.

'Guilt and introspection and doubt? It doesn't sound very cheery.'

'It's heavy going. I keep wiping it and starting again.'

'How many books have you written?'

'None.'

'So how do you survive? Financially, I

mean. No, sorry, that's nosy. Forget I asked.'

'After the accident I sued for personal damages and won. And there was the insurance money. I live off the interest.' He had no memory of all that; the Institute's lawyers had handled everything.

'Lucky you. Make a guess at the time, Mike.' It was as if she were experimenting with the diminutive to see how he reacted.

'Eleven forty-five.'

'Damn!' She sat up. 'Where's the clock? I can't see a bloody thing without my glasses. Could you put the light on, please.'

He illuminated the room and she found her glasses and looked around.

'I still can't see the clock.'

'There isn't one. I have a knack of knowing what the time is.' He took his watch from the cabinet and checked. He was one minute adrift. 'It's eleven forty-six.'

She swung her legs out of bed. 'I'm on an early in the morning; I'll have to get some sleep or I'll be a danger to the patients and Dirty Douglas will write nasty things about me.'

'You can sleep here.' He stroked the smooth skin of her back feeling the vertebrae. He was sated but he wanted her lying beside him. It must have been a long time since the last woman and he had

19

forgotten how good it felt and he wanted more of it. Not necessarily sex; just having a woman close to him was a delight. Intimacy. Her hair was a wild dark tangle.

'Don't tempt me.' She began to dress. She knew he was watching but this time she made no attempt to keep her back to him. She probably feels her body is her main asset, rather than her face, he thought.

'You're beautiful, Marianne.'

'Nice body, shame about the face.'

'I meant your face. But your body's great as well.'

She laughed and reached back to hook her bra. 'Thank you, Michael; that's very kind of you. Will you want to see me again?'

'I'll take you out for a meal tomorrow, if you're free.'

'That's a definite.' She buttoned her shirt and pushed her feet into her shoes. 'Half past seven would be good.'

'I'll call for you.'

She went to his side of the bed and sat down and they kissed. Her glasses got in the way.

'Was it good?'

'I can't remember better. I want more.'

'That sounds completely sincere.' She kissed him slowly and left. He heard the sound of her collecting the dishes and the door closing.

It would have been good to fall asleep there and then but he rose and pulled on the towelling robe and switched on the laptop.

For once he would have something interesting to report.

2

Dr Grace. Went to the library and took out a Cadfael and a Jeeves and Wooster and one about digging up WW2 aircraft from the Dutch polders. Lunch here, reading. Finished the J and W then slept for a while then carried on reading. Decided I need exercise. Marianne (?) from upstairs arrived with food. We ate then went to bed. I thought we must have done it before, from the way she seemed to expect it, but apparently it was our first time. If it's this easy to get a woman into bed I may have a new career ahead of me. Date for tomorrow night. No rage. Bannerman.

He sent the e-mail then poured a Grouse and soda. He knew it was going to be a wakeful night and settled in front of the gas fire with the Ellis Peters but kept thinking about Marianne. It was odd how the sense of desire persisted even when there was no desire left.

Without her glasses she was really quite attractive. Not beautiful, just attractive. Pleasing. Comfortable to be with. She would be nice to wake up to.

* ⋆ ⋆

The on-duty observers this time were a man and a woman. Elliot Pryce made no attempt to remember their names. It was annoying to be called to the Institute in the early hours of the morning, but the belief was that something important was happening and he had insisted that he be kept informed. The feeling of claustrophobia was making him sweat but he was determined not to let his fear show. Someone from the catering section had brought a tray of cold food and a bottle of wine but he managed only a few mouthfuls and one small glass before the cramped room made him feel squeamish. Despite his problem, the images on the playback had been erotic, especially the sequence with Bannerman and the woman groping on the couch; that had been more exciting than seeing them undress and get into bed. The cameras had been able to cope with the darkness to a certain extent, enough to show what was happening, but not in detail. The rhythmic movement under the covers had been unsatisfactory from a voyeuristic point of view. Still, the blood had been stirred. When he left the Institute he would call Shirley and make an arrangement. His beanpole wife was used to his being away for

23

days at a time and would not be surprised if he did not come home. Shirley was the obvious answer, young and stupid and obedient, impressed by authority and money, easily roused, generously built, grateful for the income and a man capable of taking his time, which was the only way he could do it nowadays.

'Tell the girl to spend more time talking to him. We need to know what he's thinking.'

'She will,' Doctor Grace said. 'This was their first time. You have to let these things develop naturally. It's dangerous to push too hard.'

'Push it. This is costing the company a fortune. We want results. I may have to put a time limit on this exercise.'

Dr Grace nodded judiciously. *Bollocks! There's too much money invested in Bannerman already and the potential rewards are immense. You're faking it, you claustrophobic prick.*

It was after one in the morning when Bannerman marked his place in the book and, on an impulse, checked his e-mail.

Bannerman. Congratulations. You might at least ask a young lady's name before bedding her. It would be good for you if you could achieve a relationship based on affection and sharing and not just sex. You

need someone to care for and to care for you.
Enjoy. Dr Grace.

He read the message and thought of killing
the connection but changed his mind. What
on earth was she doing at the Institute at this
time of night? Of course, the message could
have been diverted to her home, wherever
that was. He had assumed his e-mail would
be read when she arrived in the morning.

*Dr Grace. I think I said a couple of weeks
ago I'm getting restless, probably something
to do with Spring and the good weather and
the fact that I've been stuck here for two
months and I'd like to go on a trip, just a few
days by the sea. No rush. We'll talk about it
when you visit on Monday. Did I ever own a
Land Rover? Bannerman.*

Doctor Grace was everything Elliot Pryce
despised in company servants: a skinny
woman with serious qualifications but
restricted authority and no doubt a suburban
house and a nice little suburban garden and
an over-inflated sense of her importance. She
had the air of someone who lived with her
widowed mother. They stared at Bannerman's message on the screen.

'What do you think, Mr Pryce?' Doctor
Grace said. 'We seem to have reached a
turning point. The magazine and this query
about going on a trip to the coast and his

relationship with Marianne Shannon are all new. How do you want us to react?'

'That's your responsibility.' It was always the best response. 'You're the bloody experts. This is why we pay you so much. Start pushing. We need a result.'

Bannerman. No record of your ever owning a Land Rover, or even driving one. Maybe you had a friend owned one. Try to remember all your friends and the vehicles they owned. Where are you thinking of going on your trip? Are you going alone? Dr Grace.

Bannerman stared at the screen for a while before replying.

Dr Grace. I don't remember any friends. I certainly don't remember anyone having a Land Rover. The trip is just an idea at the moment. Spring fever. The sap rising. Probably no particular significance. Whether or not I go alone is your idea, not mine. I hadn't considered that possibility. Keep me posted on the visit. Bannerman.

The reply came back immediately.

Bannerman. Dr Leigh and I will see you Monday, usual time, and take you to lunch. Make sure your diary is up to date and copied. Dr Grace.

Bannerman switched off and took the book and a glass of milk to bed and caught the faint scent of Marianne from the sheets and

26

wanted her lying beside him.

Why? Something to do with intimacy. With not being alone. With sharing and thinking about someone other than himself and trying to please someone else and . . . And like that. It would become clear with time, hopefully. He had learned to postpone conclusions. Besides, there was the sex.

He read until he realized he had been staring at the same paragraph for some time and switched off the light.

Please, no nightmare. Not tonight.

Shannon. That was Marianne's surname. And her flatmate was Liz Parkinson.

Well done.

Now who the fuck am I?

★ ★ ★

It was raining, a grey evening, and he had read all his books. He switched on the laptop and went to the chess programme. The machine won, as it always did, even at intermediate level. The bloody thing never made a mistake. He set out to gain a one pawn advantage and after a while it thought for a long time and next thing he knew he was a pawn down and it had control of the middle of the board and he couldn't save the pawn at b2 and resigned and quit. After that

27

he played three games of Free Cell and got out twice, which was about average.

He went into Word and looked at the documents he had created over the past two months and read some of them. Investments; a few letters, none of them personal; books read and his reactions to what he'd learned; why he'd chosen the books; his reactions to the people he met; stray memories; emotions. He reported daily by e-mail what he'd been doing but the diary was supposed to be more in-depth, more personal, more like a private journal, even though the doctors always took a copy disk away with them after a visit.

His cover was that he was an author writing a mainstream novel. About guilt and intro-spection and doubt, they had advised, once the hilarity had died down. Maybe he should actually do that. He had dutifully read a couple of books about writing, just to get the jargon right in case anyone asked, and he'd actually considered writing something, but never had. With nothing between his ears but vague memories of his childhood and then the six months in the Institute since he recovered from the accident, he had little to write about. If anyone asked, Marianne for instance, he was to claim he had erased all in progress in a moment of creative exaspera-tion.

Marianne. A surprise. Had he seduced her or had she seduced him? Did it matter? How often had he thought of last night since he woke up?

He showered and applied deodorant and talc and body lotion and dressed carefully in the tan cotton suit and a blue shirt and tie, trying to anticipate the mood of the evening, trying to find the line between a forty-year-old fake author with an empty head and a rather dowdy nursing sister in her late twenties.

When he knocked on her door it was opened instantly and he was ushered inside.

'I'm almost ready,' Marianne said, looking him up and down. She was in a dressing gown, her hair and face prepared, clearly ready to adjust to whatever he was wearing.

'I wasn't sure what you fancied,' he said. 'Indian, Italian, Greek, Thai, Tibetan.'

'Tibetan?'

'If you insist, though I wouldn't recommend it. Rancid butter floating in stewed tea and slices of yak bum.'

'You're joking. Aren't you?'

'Trying to.'

She grinned at him, relieved. 'I'll be back in a minute.'

'Would you like a drink, Mike?' Liz raised a glass to indicate that she was ahead of him.

'There's gin and tonic.'

'Thank you.'

She was still in her uniform, the buttons straining, blue cotton tense across the soft bosom and wide hips.

'Marianne's nuts about you, Mike. I suppose you know that.' She handed him a full tumbler.

'No one is ever nuts about me, Liz. I'm not the sort of man a woman gets nuts about.'

'Don't put yourself down. We had a long talk last night. After what happened.'

'No secrets, apparently.'

'She was going to keep it a secret but I knew from her face what had happened and teased it out of her. She's absolutely delighted. I was delighted for both of you.'

She looked like she meant it. They smiled at each other as if they were sharing something.

'She'll be good for you, Mike. She's a lovely girl.'

'I feel good with her.'

'She's very happy with you. I mean, really happy. Don't hurt her. She's someone you can trust and confide in.'

'I won't hurt her.' *Easy to say. For all I know I'm a mass murderer.*

★　★　★

They ate Indian and talked and he mentioned he liked jazz, so afterwards Marianne took him to a pub where four men were playing and a woman singing, all badly. It was a relief when the band broke for a drink.

'Do you ever start conversations, Mike?'

'What?'

'You talk well when I can get you started, but you haven't actually initiated a subject.'

He thought about that but before he could respond she said: 'Don't get me wrong. I'm not complaining. You seem almost as shy as I am.'

'I spend too much time on my own,' he said. 'I live in a different world when I'm writing. My characters carry on conversations inside my head and I just listen. Maybe it's become a habit.'

Pretty good for someone who had never written a word of fiction.

'But you've never had anything published?'

'Not yet. It's difficult to place your first book. Especially the literary stuff like what I write.'

She grinned. 'And this is all you've ever done, all your working life?'

'No. I used to be a doctor.'

'A doctor? For heaven's sake!'

He was more surprised than she was. Usually, when he remembered something like that, it was as if he'd forgotten about it briefly and was not surprised when it came back to him. But this was so startling that he wondered if he'd got it right.

'GP?'

He shook his head, frowning. 'It was a long time ago. I forget. I mean, I don't forget, but it's not something I think about much. I guess I was in the wrong profession.'

'Where did you train?'

He didn't know. He remembered what they'd advised for situations like this.

'We're touching on a painful part of my life, Marianne. It's something I don't like to think about. Let's change the subject. I'll initiate a new subject: where are you from? That's not a London accent.'

'I'm one of your Essex girls. Sorry. What about you?'

'No, I'm not an Essex girl.'

She giggled. She'd had at least one large gin at the flat then another while they waited for a table and half a bottle of wine and now they were drinking cider.

'No, but where are you from?' she asked.

They had suggested something but he couldn't remember what. 'I'm local.'

'You don't sound like you're local. I'd have guessed at somewhere in Scotland.'

'It's probably the drink talking. Let's go

home and make love.'

'All right.'

'I hope you won't have to leave early.'

She shook her head. 'I'm on a late tomorrow. So we can make love then I can fall asleep without having to get dressed and go home first, which is my idea of the ultimate self-indulgence.' She hid a yawn. 'I think I'll become a writer and just lie around the flat all day like you and have lovers come and go and not have to worry about shifts and ward managers and rosters. I'm not trying to be possessive, but am I your only lover?'

'Yes.'

'But there must have been other women.'

'Probably.'

'Discreet silence?'

'One doesn't talk about these things.' Especially when one can't remember them.

She rested her chin on her hand and stared at him. 'You're a handsome bugger, in a slightly battered sort of way. Do you think I should get contact lenses?'

'If you see me as handsome, I'd prefer you with the glasses.'

She laughed again. 'Deal. I am ready to be made love to. I hope you've bought some condoms.'

'A dozen.'

'That'll do for tonight.'

When she was asleep he got out of bed and went quietly through to the sitting room and switched on and connected.

Dr Grace. Was I ever a doctor? Bannerman.

He stared at the sentence for a long time then erased.

Dr Grace. Spent the day reading and cleaning the flat and changing the sheets and pillowcases in anticipation of Marianne spending the night with me. We went for a curry then to a pub where I established that I like jazz but not bad jazz. Then back to my place. She's asleep in my bed now, because we didn't like the idea of having to do it quietly next door to Liz, the other girl. I am relaxed and happy but this situation doesn't seem to be doing anything for my memory. Bannerman.

He sent then went back to bed, unwilling to wait for a response. Marianne was curled up in a ball, breathing steadily, smelling of warm woman and perfume and talc. He lay close enough to feel the heat of her and stared at the pale rectangle of the window.

He tried to name the bones of the arm but the only one he could think of was the humerus. He tried to name the parts of the male reproductive system and had to accept that he knew nothing apart from the obvious.

Some doctor.

★ ★ ★

She looked good when they woke. So many women, first thing, stripped of cosmetics, were grey and blotchy and grumpy, but Marianne had colour and clear skin and made an effortless transition from sleeping to waking. She put on her glasses and looked at him.

'Hi.'

'Hi.'

'I suggest I shower first then I can make breakfast while you're doing it. Unless writers sleep till noon.'

'Bacon and eggs and tomatoes.'

'So you're not into healthy eating?'

'I eat a lot of lentil soup.'

She went naked to the bathroom and came back and began to dress. 'Your turn.'

Why did he feel guilty? And what was he feeling guilty about? Why did he want her out of the flat? Because someone might come in and see them together, but he couldn't think who it might be. And how did he know about other women being grey and blotchy and grumpy?

She was briskly efficient when he went through, serving bacon and eggs and tomatoes and toast on warmed plates. She poured strong, black coffee and she had noted that he took two sugars.

'I won't see you for a while, Mike. I have four days off and I promised to go home. I'll be leaving when I come off duty.'

'To Braintree?'

'Yes. I told you my sister's just had a baby boy and I'm desperate to see him. I'd rather spend the time with you, but I told them I'd be there.'

'I'll be here when you get back.'

'You won't go off with some other woman?'

'Well, there's Liz . . . '

'That's not funny.'

'Yes it is.'

'It's not.' She stopped with the fork halfway to her mouth. 'Shit. My insecurity is showing. I'm very much aware of what I look like, and I've no self-confidence when it comes to personal relationships. Forget it.'

'I'll be here, Marianne. Waiting for you.'

'You sound like you really mean it.'

He nodded. 'I mean it.'

She was trying to be convinced but wasn't quite managing it. He felt sorry for her but couldn't think what to say.

Elliot Pryce couldn't believe what he was hearing.

'On leave? What do you mean, on bloody leave?'

'Her sister's had a baby ... ' Dr Grace said.

'I don't care if her bloody sister's had a bloody football team! Where she should be is in Bannerman's bloody bed, getting the idiot to talk, not farting around in bloody Essex!'

'It's all carefully calculated,' Dr Grace said, trying to sound authoritative and professional. 'Separation at this time is good applied psychology. Bannerman has been guided into a new emotional scenario and now we need the shock effect of separation to reinforce the emotional pressure. Liz Parkinson is on hand to make the most of his reaction. When Marianne comes back Bannerman will be desperate to confide in her. And it's time for Marianne to stop being a dowdy little nobody and resort to being a very attractive young woman. The glasses are deliberately unbecoming, the hairstyle is deliberately unflattering, the clothes are carefully selected to do her no favours. That way Bannerman was less likely to be suspicious when she came on to him. He might have had difficulty accepting the same eagerness from a beautiful young woman. With Marianne looking so ordinary he had no reason to suspect anything.'

Pryce wiped the sweat off his forehead. He wanted out of this bloody tomb.

'I want to know what's happening as it happens.'

Dr Grace watched him leave and exhaled slowly.

Bullshit baffles brains. Is that the correct phrase? Psychological pap persuades prats.

★   ★   ★

Bannerman drove Marianne to the station and carried her bag and saw her to her seat and sat opposite until the last moment. She looked depressed. He checked his watch and rose and bent to kiss her and she gripped his arms tightly.

'Wait for me, Mike.'

'I'll be waiting.'

★   ★   ★

Dr Grace. Check on Marianne Shannon of this address. Nursing sister, age 28, born Braintree, Essex. 5′6″, about ten stone, slim, very good figure, dark hair shoulder length, olive complexion, glasses, brown eyes, single, shares a flat with Elizabeth Parkinson, also a sister, same hospital.

He hesitated, feeling guilty and somehow a traitor. His instinct was to trust Marianne. She was so perfectly natural, so vulnerable, so understandable, so invigorating, so easy to be close to, so exciting.

She asks a lot of personal questions, but I suppose that's natural. I suspect I'm having difficulty accepting that any attractive young woman is interested in me. Bannerman.

★　★　★

Greying hair suited Dr Grace. It went with her height and her thin body and her natural elegance, giving her authority.

'Hello, Michael.'

'Hello, Doctor. Come in. Hello, Dr Leigh, how are you?'

A flurry of conventions as he took their raincoats and ushered them to the couch and the armchair in front of the coffee table. He served coffee.

'How are you feeling, Mike?' Dr Leigh asked. 'You're looking well.'

'I feel great.'

'Would that have something to do with having a bit of romance in your life?'

'I dare say that has helped, yes.' He hoped they weren't going to ask for details.

Dr Grace opened a file. There was a photograph stapled to the top left corner of a sheet of paper.

'In response to your query, Michael,' she said. 'Marianne Margaret Shannon, age 28, born Braintree, Essex, 1972. Local schools then did her nursing training here in London. She seems a thoroughly nice young lady. No intellectual, but good grades at school and she sailed through her nursing training and several additional courses. We don't have a lot on her private life, of course, but, really, you could just about write it yourself. No hidden husbands or children, no police record; well thought of at the hospital, although there's apparently some friction between her and one of the ward managers. No major problems. Without wanting to sound like a Victorian mother, what are your intentions?'

'I think I've achieved all my intentions.'

'Sex, you mean.'

'Yes.'

'I see.' It always sounded ominous when Dr Angela Grace said 'I see' and wrote something in her notebook. 'When Marianne first arrived at your door that evening, what was your reaction? Were you surprised, or did you accept the situation?'

'It seemed natural. She'd made a meal for her flatmate then remembered she wasn't coming home.'

'I was thinking of the sex. You thought perhaps it had happened before?'

Bannerman shrugged. 'She seemed natural, at ease, so I responded. I've learned to do that. If someone seems to remember something I go with it. The message I was getting was that we had made love before and I was . . . hell, I was randy. She didn't resist. I really thought we'd done it before and I'd forgotten.'

'Had you ever eaten Italian food before?'

'Yes. Macaroni, here. I made it.'

'I mean, did it bring back any specific memories? About eating out with a young woman in a restaurant, for instance?'

'No.'

Norman Leigh had his own file. 'Anything further on the Land Rover magazine, Mike? Anything come back to you?'

'Nothing. I've been through it a third time but it might as well be silk screen printing or chiropody or bulls' pizzles for fun and profit. I can see what they're on about but only as a disinterested outsider. There was nothing I remembered.'

'But you asked for the magazine, specifically.'

41

'Without knowing it exists.'

'Had you seen a Land Rover in the street, perhaps?'

'Not that I remember.'

'Did you see the magazine on the shelf in the shop, even unconsciously?'

'No. It was hidden behind some other motoring magazines.'

Dr Leigh nodded and glanced at Dr Grace and she looked slightly embarrassed.

'When you and Miss Shannon . . . Tell us about that. Did you . . . approach her?'

He gave them the gist of it, keeping it as matter-of-fact as possible.

'You thought you'd done it before?' Dr Leigh said.

'I assumed we had. I was misled by the way she seemed to expect it. As if it wasn't the first time. My memory told me we hadn't made love but the actuality seemed to suggest otherwise and, of course, I can't trust my memory. So I went with the flow.'

The doctors glanced at each other and he guessed that part of the problem might be their ages and conventions. It was impossible to imagine the spinsterish Dr Angela Grace delivering lasagne uninvited and happily having her tits groped shortly afterwards. And fat little Dr Norman Leigh looked as if he had been bald since his early twenties and had probably married a nice young lady arranged by his mother.

'Young women these days are very direct,' Bannerman said. 'I've read about it. And it seems to be true.'

Leigh nodded as if he understood. 'Are you still carrying the knife and the cosh?'

'Yes.'

'Have you at any time felt a need to use them?'

'No.'

'Nightmares?'

'Not since the one I reported about two weeks ago.'

Dr Grace finished making notes. 'You've been talking about going on a trip. Tell us about that.'

'That's all new, all remembered from the start,' Bannerman said. 'I feel cooped up here. I want to get out, get some fresh air, walk along a beach, get some exercise. I think the good weather is an influence.'

'You mentioned the coast. Why the coast?'

'I don't know. Because that's where people go for fresh air and exercise, I suppose. I don't think there's anything more to it than that, Except . . . '

'Except what?'

He shrugged. 'There may be more to it than that. Please don't ask me to be more specific, because I won't be able to answer your questions, but I have something at the back of my mind about a sea and a shore and rocks and sand which keeps popping up at odd moments.'

'Are these memories consistent?'

'It's the same sea, the same beach, the same rocks.'

'Have you made definite plans?'

He shook his head. 'Getting the car serviced may have been prompted by the idea, but that's as far as I've got. I haven't been looking at road maps or brochures. But I want to go. And I may want to take Marianne with me.'

'All right. Keep us informed. Strip, please.'

3

He stripped and they went over him carefully, took his blood pressure and a urine sample, examined his retinas, tested his reflexes, listened to his heart and lungs, drew some blood, looked at his nails and the palms of his hands.

'Now the questions, Michael. Don't think about your responses, just tell us whatever comes to you first.'

He leant back and closed his eyes. There were times, when they did this test, that he was tempted to throw in a few ridiculous answers just to give them something to think about, but he never did. After all, they were trying to help him and he was grateful.

Twenty minutes later Dr Leigh said: 'That's it, thanks, Mike.'

'Was I ever a doctor?'

They stared at him. 'Why do you ask, Michael?' Dr Grace asked.

He thought back. 'I'm not sure. Something I said to Marianne. But I can't remember the names of the bones in the arm. I tried.'

'What do you mean, something you said? Did you have a memory?'

'No, I just came right out and said it. I said I'd been a doctor. But I don't know why I said it.'

'Where's your pancreas?'

He pointed vaguely at his abdomen.

'Pituitary gland?'

He shrugged helplessly.

She pressed a finger under his right collar bone and he jerked away. 'Which nerve is that?'

'No idea.'

Dr Grace glanced at her colleague. 'You may have been a doctor, Michael. We just don't know. Although I'd have expected you to remember at least some of the stuff they would have drummed into you at med school. Let us know if you get any more pointers in the same direction.'

He copied his diary to disk for them then they went for lunch at the Running Fox. It was a convention established over the two months he had been in the flat and they had reached the stage of being uncomfortable with each other. They all ordered the chicken salad and drank one glass of warm white wine and left half the food uneaten.

'Anything new for me?' Bannerman asked. 'Are we getting anywhere?'

'We mustn't give up hope, Mike,' Dr Leigh said. 'We're making progress. Every little bit of information is a step in the right direction.'

So they weren't getting anywhere. He looked at their institutional faces and felt a surge of irritation.

'I'm getting pissed off with being the equivalent of an experimental rat in a maze.'

'We're trying to help you, Michael,' Dr Grace said. 'You're the one with the problem. We're doing all we can to solve it. You're certainly not an experiment.'

'Sorry. You still haven't found any reference to me anywhere?'

'Not yet. We have people searching, but no luck yet.'

'I don't understand how I could just be hauled out of a wrecked car eight months ago with nothing to show who I am and where I worked and what family I have. Surely someone notified the police that I'd gone missing.'

Dr Grace nodded and pursed her bloodless lips; the action drew attention to the fine grey hairs around her mouth. 'We've been through this, Michael. We had people make all the usual checks, but no joy. There are all sorts of possibilities: maybe you'd just come home from abroad, for instance. Maybe you'd never had a job. Maybe you had deliberately created a new identity for yourself. Maybe you were between jobs and have no family.'

'The answers are up there, Mike,' Dr Leigh said, pointing to Bannerman's head. 'Everything you need to know is locked away in your mind. We're helping all we can, but in the long run you're going to have to solve this mystery yourself.'

He waved to them as they drove off in Dr Leigh's polite little French car and walked back to the flat feeling depressed and angry. So far as they were concerned, despite their protestations of concern, he had no life outwith their files. To them he was not a human being, a man with problems; to them he was an interesting case study in need of a conclusion, hopefully capable of being worked up into a joint article for publication.

Which left him with no life of his own worth mentioning. He was a lonely and isolated man with no family, no friends, no job, no purpose, no past, no clear future. He didn't even have a character, really; losing his years of experience had left him unsure about how he should react to what happened around him, what his attitudes once were, what he should believe in. There were times when the difference between right and wrong was unclear. This was partly why he read so much and so widely, sometimes choosing books from the long list supplied by the Institute, sometimes picking at random from the library shelves. He was trying to pack into a few months everything he had absorbed over many years but had forgotten.

I'm not totally alone, now. There's Marianne.

He felt a sudden powerful longing for her, but it was not for her body. He wanted her to be with him as a person, someone to communicate with, someone to talk with and laugh with and share with. Someone who actually cared that he was alive.

★   ★   ★

Dr Grace and Dr Leigh stopped at Elliot Pryce's office on the way back to the Institute, as instructed. They had to wait almost an hour before being summoned to the opulent office. There was no offer of coffee.

'Well? Anything?' Pryce seemed more relaxed in his own environment, marginally less aggressive, but his manners had not improved. Dr Grace felt the sense of relief which came from having something definite to report.

'He asked if he was ever a doctor.'

'Ah! So he remembers that, at least.'

'Not quite. But he's remembered something which has made him wonder. It's a

49

giant step forward. A process has started.'

'Can't you accelerate this bloody process?'

'That would be dangerous. The mind protects itself, remember; that's why there's a huge blank. We have to rely on his mind releasing the information gradually. If it all comes back in a rush we might lose him permanently. He could, quite simply, lose his mind.'

Pryce looked at Dr Leigh as if seeking a second opinion. Leigh nodded judiciously. He considered himself academically superior to his colleague, but she had the seniority so she could take the flak.

'There are encouraging signs,' he said. 'Bannerman's thinking is logical and intelligent, given the huge blank in his memory. He has learned and retained a great deal since he was brought back from Africa and came out of the coma. Physically, he has recovered completely from what happened. Now, all we can do is what we're doing — give him time and space in the community, where he is open to all sorts of stimuli, and hope that he will remember.'

'So I can report to the board that you're making progress.' Elliot Pryce sounded like a man under pressure.

'Yes,' Dr Grace said. 'We're quite pleased by this development.' She saw the dissatisfaction gathering on Pryce's narrow face.

'There's something else, something which may turn out to be even more significant. He has an urge to go to the coast.'

Elliot Pryce raised his hands in mock excitement. 'The coast! How exciting! Let's all club together and buy him a bucket and a bloody spade!'

'When he was a boy he lived with his father for several years on an island in Orkney, after his parents split up. His father still lives there. We think that's what he may be remembering. It's much too early to say, but this could be the breakthrough we've been looking for.'

'So when do you expect . . . ?'

'There's no anticipated time. We don't expect anything. It will be a miracle if we succeed.' Let the bastards know what they're asking, Dr Grace thought. Make sure they know that failure is almost inevitable, so it won't be my fault. And how clever I'll have been if we succeed.

* * *

Bannerman put down the book and went to the sideboard and poured a whisky and soda. The feeling of depression and anger had lingered throughout the afternoon; it would have been good if Marianne had been on hand to help him forget. He glanced at the

51

door, imagining her standing there with the tray in her hand . . .

He frowned and stared at the door for a long time then put down the glass and switched on the laptop and went back through his e-mails, puzzled, wondering if this was just another example of his unreliable memory.

Dr Grace. Went to the library and took out a Cadfael and a Jeeves and Wooster and one about digging up WW2 aircraft from the Dutch polders. Lunch here, reading. Finished the J and W then slept for a while then carried on reading. Marianne (?) from upstairs arrived with food. We ate then went to bed. I thought we must have done it before, from the way she seemed to expect it, but apparently it was our first time. If it's this easy to get a woman into bed I may have a new career ahead of me. Date for tomorrow night. No rage.

He'd been right. *Marianne (?) from upstairs arrived with food.*

He had said nothing about lasagne or pasta. But Dr Grace had known what he and Marianne had eaten.

He closed the laptop and felt a prickle of fear.

★ ★ ★

Marianne called from Braintree on the Tuesday morning and Bannerman arranged to collect her from the station. They kissed awkwardly on the platform then he carried her bag to the car.

'So how's your new nephew?'

'He's lovely. Bald as a billiard ball, beautiful blue eyes, tiny fingers. Still faithful?'

'What? Oh. Yes, still faithful.'

'I swore I wasn't going to say anything. I didn't want to come on like the jealous lover. Forget I said that.'

They bought a pizza and went straight to his flat and ate and drank a few cans of cider from his fridge and he smiled at photographs of a child who looked like every child ever born. Marianne's sister was very like her and very attractive.

'You've said all the right things, Mike, but I suspect I'm boring you.'

He shook his head vigorously. 'Not at all.'

'But you're very quiet.'

'Personal problems. You're not the cause — you're the antidote. Can you get some time off?'

'No. I had to argue till I was blue in the face to get an extra two days to add to my days off so I could go home. That's me till July. Why?'

'I want to go on a trip. A few days out of

here. It would be great if you could come with me.'

'Where are you thinking of going?'

'I don't know. The coast, somewhere.'

'A hotel? I'd love that. It's my ambition to be made love to in a hotel while unmarried. There's a marvellous sense of sin about it. Can't you postpone till July?'

'We'll do it properly in July. Two weeks. Wales, Scotland, Ireland, anywhere you want. But I need a break now. A change of scene. I've been thinking about it for a while.'

'To help you with the book?'

He hadn't thought of that. 'Yes. I need a change of scene to give me some ideas.'

'When are you leaving?'

'I don't know. Soon.'

'How long for?'

'A few days. Maybe a week.'

She eased herself into his arms and hugged him tightly. 'Delay for a bit. I'll see what I can manage.'

They went to bed and made love and fell asleep wrapped together. When he woke in the morning she was dressed and sitting beside him on the bed, running her fingers through his hair.

'You won't go off without me?'

'What?' He was confused.

'Your trip. You won't just go off without

telling me, will you?'

'Of course not.'

She was gone when he woke again, and when he knocked at her door there was no answer. He made toast and coffee and wondered if he could trust her.

Who knew about the lasagne? He did, and he hadn't mentioned it to anyone. Marianne had known. Marianne could have told Liz about it. And now Dr Grace knew. Which meant that Dr Leigh knew and it was in the files, which didn't matter. What mattered was how the information had reached Dr Grace.

It had to mean that Marianne and presumably Liz had been sent to watch him. And that had to mean that Marianne had been instructed to get him into bed with her. So — all the whispered words and the intimacy and the passion had been faked.

Hers, but not his.

He stared at the butter congealing on the cold toast and felt ashamed and embarrassed and angry and deeply hurt.

No. He couldn't believe Marianne could have done that to him. Her feelings were all too obvious. She was a plainish girl of 28, unmarried, no boyfriend, no sex, missing out, maybe worried about the years slipping away. And she was so important to him.

There had to be another explanation.

But if Marianne wasn't spying on him, then how the hell . . . ?

Maybe it was all a mistake. Maybe he'd forgotten something. Maybe he'd misunderstood something. Maybe he had said something to the doctors but forgotten.

He looked round the room. Maybe there were microphones . . . Maybe there were cameras . . .

★ ★ ★

Marianne and Liz were having coffee with Dr Grace in the staff restaurant when the phone rang. Dr Grace listened and frowned then said: 'That was Martin. He wants to see me urgently. You'd better come too.'

In the basement, Martin Brown indicated the screens. 'We think he's on to us.'

They looked at the images of Michael Bannerman in his kitchen. He made a cup of instant coffee then went to the armchair beside the fireplace in the sitting room and sat down and began to read.

'Looks all right to me,' Dr Grace said. 'He's not doing anything odd.'

'It's what he's not doing,' the technician said. 'Since about half past nine this morning he hasn't burped or farted or picked his nose or gone to the lavatory. He went out at 11.06 and drove to the library and took out three books, but Letitia says he also went to the lavatory there. He's never done that before. He's acting like someone who knows there are cameras in his flat. Watch this. John? The edited highlights, please.'

John Valance ran a tape. It showed Michael Bannerman using a pair of nail scissors to trim his moustache and beard with the help of a small mirror held in one hand.

'So he's trimming his beard. He's done that before,' Dr Grace said.

'On previous occasions he used the mirror on the wall in the bathroom,' Valance said. 'This time he's using the mirror to hide the fact that he's searching for cameras. There! See that?'

Bannerman's eyes were reflected in the mirror. They seemed to focus on the camera hidden in the cornice in one corner of the sitting room then moved away. Dr Grace had examined the setup before Bannerman was moved to the flat and knew that the tiny lens was invisible behind a crack in the plaster, but it was all too evident that Bannerman was suspicious.

'I'm not convinced . . . '

'Watch.'

Bannerman moved to the bedroom and lay

down on his back on the bed and appeared to be trying to sleep.

'Watch his eyes. They're not fully closed. There! That's when he finds the lens. Now he really closes his eyes and pretends to sleep. Now this.'

In his bathroom, Bannerman washed his face and then combed his moustache and beard and appeared to be examining the effects of his efforts with the scissors. His narrowed eyes flickered away from his reflection to the top corners of the room.

'I'm not sure if he spotted anything that time,' Valance said, switching off the video, 'but the point is that he was searching.'

'He knows,' Brown said. 'He hasn't spotted all of them, but one is enough. He knows he's being observed, and he's clever enough to disguise the fact. If he'd just farted a couple of times and sat on the bog and played with his willie we wouldn't have noticed. I bet you, by tomorrow, he'll have worked it out that he's giving himself away and he'll start burping and farting and picking his nose again. But he won't play with himself. No one ever does, in this situation.'

Dr Grace looked at Marianne. 'He may suspect you as well. Whatever has made him suspicious, you'll be part of it. Can you handle that?'

'Yes. But I may not get the chance. If he knows he's being watched he's not likely to get amorous.'

'So get him into your own bedroom,' Liz said. 'He'll assume that's been bugged as well.'

'Damn!' Dr Grace picked up a phone and pressed a key.

'We have a major problem, Norman. Get down to the basement.'

★　★　★

Bannerman walked round the park, slowly, hands in trouser pockets, watching without making it obvious. The black woman followed on foot on the other side of the railings then got into a Ford Fiesta and the car tracked him, stopping and starting, moving a hundred yards at a time. It was skilfully done; if he hadn't been looking for it he would not have noticed.

The flat has been fitted with cameras, there's a car seemingly on permanent watch, and Marianne may be one of them, a plant. Probably Liz as well. Why? Why am I so bloody important to them?

He left the park and crossed the road to a small pub he had never been in before and ordered a whisky and soda with ice and found a seat in a corner. Immediately, the black woman and a white woman entered and bought drinks and took a table at the other end of the bar and became engrossed in conversation. When he emptied his glass and rose they stopped talking and drank up and prepared to leave. He glanced back when he reached the corner and they were getting into the Ford Fiesta.

★   ★   ★

'You're going to have to turn up the heat, Marianne,' Dr Grace said. 'He's clearly getting a lot of pleasure out of your company; he's relaxed with you, he likes you, you don't scare him. You did a marvellous job of looking ordinary and vulnerable and a little bit dowdy and he had no trouble accepting your eagerness to get into bed with him. Now you have to come over like a young woman with new confidence, eager to please, wanting to hold on to a man. Lose the glasses and that awful hairstyle. A touch of make-up, some flattering clothes, sexy underwear. On expenses.'

'No problem. But what if he suspects me?'

'I don't think he will. He has the cameras to worry him and he won't want to suspect you. He won't want to lose you. You're his first woman in eight months.'

Bannerman lay in bed in the darkness and listened to the quiet knock at the flat door. It was repeated, louder, and he heard the handle being tried. After that, silence, and then the sound of a door opening and closing upstairs. He stared at the pale rectangle of the window.

Could they see him in the dark? Had they watched him making love to Marianne? Christ! And they must have watched him groping her on the couch, his hand inside her shirt. And they'd stripped naked before getting into bed and the light had been on at that stage and he'd had a pretty obvious erection.

He squirmed in the bed, trying to escape the image and the knowledge that people somewhere had observed his desire.

Is this all just paranoia? Maybe there's nothing behind the cracks in the plaster except more plaster. Maybe I said something to the doctors then forgot. Could Marianne have done what she did knowing it was being transmitted on CCTV? The second time, when she was on top, naked, the covers thrown back, moaning and sighing . . . No, she couldn't have known. She would never have done all that if she'd known it was being watched on screens somewhere by men with cynical eyes. And she'd gone naked to the shower and come back and dressed and kissed him and spoken words of love . . .

Marianne was as much a victim as he was.

I can't even go for a bloody piss. I haven't burped or farted or gone to the lavatory since I became suspicious. Will they spot that? They're presumably experts. They probably have a Home Office manual which describes how to recognize when a victim suspects he is under surveillance: *'Watch out for a change in behaviour. In the privacy of his own home the average British male farts noisily on average once every two hours, burps once an hour, picks his nose twice a day and fondles his private parts whenever he sits on the toilet. When he does not display this behaviour it should be assumed that he is aware that he is under observation'.*

Something like that. It wasn't a joke.

He swung out of bed and went naked to the bathroom and switched on the light and sat down. It was desperately difficult not to glance up at the crack where the wall met the ceiling, and even more difficult to do what he needed to do. He should have brought something to read . . .

I'm going bloody mad.

What if I went to a doctor and said, Hello,

I'm already receiving treatment for a mental problem and now I'm convinced there are cameras and microphones hidden all over my flat, a car tailing me, two women following me into a pub, an attractive woman throwing herself at me so she can get into my bed and my mind. What's your diagnosis please?

Paranoia, you frigging loony.

He went to the kitchen then back to bed.

I'm suffering from amnesia and yet my only explanation for Dr Grace knowing Marianne brought me lasagne is cameras and spies and surveillance. Come on, you stupid bastard, get sensible. It's either paranoia or a severe case of self-importance.

★ ★ ★

Dr Leigh took the call at home.

'It's OK, Doctor. Bannerman doesn't suspect anything.'

'You're sure?'

'Positive. He just went to the bathroom naked and crapped, then he drank a glass of milk and rifted.'

'Thank you. Call Dr Grace at home and let her know.' *You won't be interrupting anything of any importance.*

Dr Grace phoned him a few minutes later. 'We seem to have got away with it this time,

Norman, but we're going to have to accelerate the process. The board isn't going to tolerate a long delay. This whole exercise is costing a fortune.'

'But the potential profits are immense; the time is justified.'

'It's getting to the stage where it would be cheaper to send in someone else to do the work all over again rather than wait for Bannerman to remember. That's what Pryce just told me over the phone. He called me just after eleven, the bastard.'

Norman Leigh felt relief that Elliot Pryce had not called him at home late at night, but resentful that Pryce had called Angela and not him. 'We can't accelerate the process. Not safely.'

'Maybe safely doesn't matter any more.'

They had been working together for fifteen years and felt a deep hatred for each other but knew that success was dependent on their joint efforts.

'Perhaps,' Leigh said, 'perhaps it's time to start exposing him to his past. Perhaps we should prepare a schedule of stimuli.'

'That sounds suitably scientific, Norman. Go on.'

'Something prompted him to tell Marianne he was a doctor. Instead of denying that, maybe we should let him know he's right,

64

that he was a doctor, maybe even suggest a visit to Edinburgh in the hope that something will trigger a connection.'

'He shared a flat with two other students. He played rugby for the university. He had several girlfriends. He frequented several pubs. Plenty there for him to remember. Is that what you're suggesting?'

'Yes. It's just a matter of getting him there without making him wonder why.'

'Marianne. Get her to come in again.'

Don't give me orders, you dried-up old fart.

★　★　★

The knock came at the door in the middle of the evening.

'Hi, Mike. How are you?' She stood in the opening with a look of hesitancy on her face.

'Fine. Come in.' He closed the door behind her and held out his arms and they kissed and clung together.

'I knocked at your door last night, but you didn't answer.' She sounded hurt.

'I was here, but I think I fell asleep at one stage. You should have made more noise.'

'Doesn't matter. Except I had to spend the evening listening to Liz moaning about her non-existent love life instead of getting on with my own. You should have given me a shout when you woke up.'

'I thought of it, but I wasn't sure how you'd react.'

'You should know by now. You're the only thing of any importance in my life. If I get contact lenses, would that make me more attractive?'

He looked down at her anxious face and the annoying glasses. 'Your glasses hide your eyes, and you have beautiful eyes. Go for it. I'll pay for them.'

He imagined people watching all this on CCTV somewhere, listening to what he was saying, laughing at him, then remembered his decision that he was just being paranoid.

'All right.' She unbuttoned his shirt and kissed his chest and moved against him. 'I'm burning up. So are you. I can feel it.'

'So let's do something about that.'

It was better now that they knew each other and had more control over what was happening. Afterwards, he lay on his back with his arms spread-eagled across the bed, the covers pushed down, enjoying the afterglow and the cool air on his skin. She lay beside him, one hand gently stroking his stomach.

'You're a very good lover, Mike. Very

skilful. I won't ask where you learned how to do it.'

'Can't remember, anyway.'

'Bollocks. How could you forget that?'

Good question. He didn't have an answer. 'It was a long time ago.'

'Dirty Douglas is being moved to another ward. There's a chance I could get some time off. Do you still want to go on a trip?'

'Yes.' That was true. He had become increasingly determined to go somewhere by the sea and walk on sand and gravel and hear the waves crashing and feel the wind on his face. It was somehow important.

'I'm meeting my new ward manager tomorrow.'

'Tell her . . . '

'It's a him.'

'Tell him your entire future with a certain novelist depends on your being made love to at frequent intervals for a week in a marine environment.'

She giggled. 'I'll try to remember all that.'

'Seduce me.'

'I don't know how.'

'Every woman knows.'

'I'll see what I can do.'

He felt her move around his body and knew that she could not do all this knowing she was appearing on a screen somewhere.

'Do you like that?'
'Don't stop.'

★   ★   ★

'We've arranged to wait until after my period then we'll go. He's installed an atlas in his laptop and we've gone over it and so far it's Holy Island then St Andrews then Loch Ness then wherever we can find a place to stay on the west coast. Scourie, Ullapool. I forget the names. We'll just play it by ear.'

'Good. Well done, Marianne.' Dr Grace pushed a sheet of paper across the desk. 'This is the list of stimuli we want you to introduce into the conversation, starting now. Memorize then destroy; he mustn't see it. We'll be watching his reactions on CCTV, of course, but when you're off on your trip you'll have to observe and report. And it's important that you spend some time in Edinburgh.'

'Why?'

'That's where he trained as a doctor, mostly at the Western General.' She offered a second sheet. 'The addresses of two flats he lived in, with the dates. The names of people he shared with, close friends, girlfriends, favourite pubs and restaurants, a brief history of his life at that time. Again, he mustn't see this. We want him presented with a range of things which might help him remember, and we want you to note his responses. Can you persuade him to spend a day in Edinburgh?'

'Should be possible. What if he suddenly remembers everything all at once? How will he behave? Will he become violent?'

Dr Grace sat back in her chair and made a face. 'We don't know, Marianne. It would be a major shock to him. He might even collapse. Certainly, he would be confused and disorientated and shocked. Don't worry about that. You're well trained and you have your pager: hit the panic button and someone will arrive immediately, wherever you are.'

Marianne blinked and rubbed her eyes; it was taking time to get used to the contact lenses.

'I'd hate to see him get hurt. He's a nice guy and it's not his fault.'

'You're playing a role, Marianne. Never forget that. Don't get too close to him.'

'I'm sleeping with him.'

'That's not what I mean, and you know it. It's most unlikely that he has a future of any kind. His present condition is artificial. There's a very good chance that opening his mind will leave him permanently damaged. In self-defence, don't get too close to him emotionally.'

Marianne scanned the two sheets of paper. 'I'll memorize this lot and return the papers to you before I leave tonight.'

'What are you doing about changing your appearance?'

'I spent today buying clothes and I have an appointment with a hairdresser for tomorrow. If he doesn't respond to the new knickers he's not the man I think he is.'

4

Elliot Pryce sat on a hard chair in the office shared by Dr Grace and Dr Leigh and pointedly ignored the coffee the skinny woman had poured for him.

'He's off on bloody holiday? At the company's expense? With a woman also provided at the company's expense? How do I get a job like that? I'd love a job like that. I could do that forever.'

'This is a major advance,' Dr Grace said, glancing across at Dr Leigh and knowing the fat little wank was going to leave her to struggle on her own. 'Bannerman has displayed a persistent urge to visit the coast and we need to know why. It may relate to his father, but we're not sure. And Marianne, the woman he has with him, is going to try to get him to visit Edinburgh, which is where he trained as a doctor. We've provided her with information about his years at medical school and she'll make sure he's confronted with a range of places he may remember. It's our opinion that we may be on the verge of accelerating his recovery. Which is what you've been demanding.'

Pryce smiled without humour; it was almost a sneer. *He has a face built for sneering,* Dr Grace thought. *He has a face ideally suited for grinding a heel into.*

'Don't even try to make it sound like it's my idea, Doctor. You're the experts; your job is to advise me. Letting him wander off on a subsidised fuck-fest is your idea, not mine. I'll be happy to arrange for you to meet the Executive to explain yourself if it all goes wrong.'

He gave her a threatening look then glanced at Norman Leigh and offered a tiny smile.

Divide and terrify.

★ ★ ★

I should get cards printed, Bannerman thought, staring at the rear of the truck he had been following for twenty minutes in the middle lane. *Then, when someone asks for my name and I can't remember I'll just reach for a card and pass it over with a quick glance to remind myself.*

Not a silly idea. Sensible. Logical. He had no trouble thinking logically, intelligently, planning ahead, constructing a course of action. It was going backwards that was the problem, looking into a past that was

72

uniformly black and unknowable; it meant that almost everything he did had to be done for the first time. No shortcuts, no habits, no routine. His life began roughly eight months back, but not at any particular moment. The first two months were erratic, a mixture of light and darkness, remembering and forgetting, strange faces, books new to him but which he later learned he had read before. That was why the daily diary on the laptop was so important; he went back over it frequently, reinforcing his memories, still surprised at the passages he couldn't remember remembering, let alone writing.

Perhaps he'd be able to remember his own name if he knew what it really was. They said it was Michael Bannerman, but maybe it was something else. Maybe that was why he had so much trouble with it.

He remembered one of the sessions at the Institute.

'*What sort of person am I?*'

'*What do you mean, Michael?*'

'*My character. Am I an introvert or an extrovert? Kind or selfish? Aggressive or tolerant? Loving or distant? Talkative or silent? Things like that. I don't know.*'

Dr Grace and Dr Leigh had exchanged looks then she had thought for a long moment before replying.

'We're unable to tell you, Michael. We don't know. Everything we know is what you yourself already know. You were found badly smashed up in a traffic accident near Bristol, dressed very casually, no wallet, no papers, nothing to identify you except an inscription on the back of your watch saying: 'To Mike Bannerman with thanks'. You were a passenger, not the driver, and it looks as if you were just getting a lift. The driver was dead. He was traced and everyone who knew him and spoke to him that day was questioned but no one knew anything about you. He was a sales rep travelling from Birmingham to various calls in the Bristol area. The police did everything they could to trace your family or your job or your home, but failed. Your photograph was published, but your face was damaged and no one recognized you. You were in a coma for six weeks and when you became conscious again you were suffering from severe amnesia; you could remember fairly well up to the age of about ten but then it was just a matter of isolated and rather meaningless scraps of memory. We've been trying to put you together ever since.'

'We don't know anything about your character, Mike,' Dr Leigh had said. 'You're a bit of blank sheet. Maybe, with time, your *true character will surface along with your memory.'*

'What happened to the watch?'

'It was smashed; I imagine it was dumped.'

Bannerman glanced across at Marianne, asleep in the passenger seat. It was still a shock to see her without her glasses; the contact lenses seemed to have given her confidence and she had been to a hairdresser and now her dark hair was cut short and he could see her eyebrows and eyelashes and the fine cheek-bones. She was actually very attractive. Her new habit of blinking and rubbing her eyes would soon vanish.

She was, beautiful. A major surprise. It seemed as if their relationship had given her the confidence to make the most of herself. And the tight tops were new, as if she'd suddenly realized she had a figure and had become confident enough to show it.

Her suggestion that they spend a day in Edinburgh was a very minor annoyance. He had no interest in a strange city; he wanted to get to the coast, somewhere in Scotland, somewhere . . . He couldn't even remember the moment when he realized it had to be Scotland.

He'd know when he found it. Perhaps. A windy place with waves breaking into white foam on rocks; short grass with tiny white flowers; the cry of birds.

A place with a desperate sense of loss.

★ ★ ★

They spent the night at a hotel below Bamburgh Castle; Marianne shyly asked for a proper dinner in the dining room rather than a bar supper.

'It's my first time being sinful in a hotel with a lover,' she whispered across the table. 'I want to do it properly.'

He smiled at her excitement. 'So do I.'

Afterwards they went for a walk before going upstairs to make love and then push the Downie away while they cooled off.

'There's something specially exciting about sleeping in a different bed, Mike. Do you feel it?'

'Yes. Different bounce.'

'That's not what I mean, pig.'

'I don't know what you mean. This is only the third bed I've ever slept in, at least that I remember. The one at the Institute, my own bed, now here. I haven't even slept in your bed.'

They had opened the curtains before going to bed and he could see her sitting up and looking at him.

'Go on, Mike. What's the Institute? I

guessed there was something odd about you, something to do with your memory, but I didn't like to ask. I was hoping you'd tell me when you were ready. Is it anything I should worry about?'

He stroked her back. 'No. I told you about the car crash. I was in a coma for six weeks then came to suffering from amnesia. They say it should all come back in time.'

'You're not going to pass out while driving or anything like that, are you?'

'I haven't blacked out since I woke up. I do have a nightmare every so often, but then I wake up and that's it.'

She shivered and lay down and he pulled the quilt over them. She nestled close and wrapped an arm and a leg around him.

'If there's anything I can do to help, just ask, though I can't think of anything,' she said, then, after a few minutes: 'Am I your first woman since the accident?'

'Yes. For all I know you may be my first woman ever.'

'I doubt it. But I like the idea. 'There's no love like a man's first and a woman's last'. If you can't remember, then that sort of means I'm your first. That's quite exciting.'

'I've nothing to compare myself with. I don't know if I'm any good.'

'You're the best. Not that I'm an expert,

you understand; it's not as if I've had a mass of lovers. But you're very good.'

'It's all instinct. And what I've seen on television. And books. And responding to what you do.'

'I think you've got the hang of it, Mike.'

★   ★   ★

In the morning he drove across the causeway to Holy Island and they walked around, looking at the huts made from upturned boats and the ruined church and the old houses. He spent a long time walking on the beach, fascinated by the sand and the dried seaweed and the line of rubbish along the high-water mark, the smell and sound of the sea, the quality of the light, the immense sky, the distant castle. He stopped and stared at a lobster pot, feeling something niggling at the back of his mind: rusting wire, blue rope, chicken netting. Had he been here before? But lobster pots probably looked the same from Dungeness to Shetland. He walked back towards the car reluctantly, knowing they had to be over the causeway before the tide came in. When he licked his lips he tasted salt and a memory came flooding back but stopped before he could get hold of it.

He watched Marianne. She was a woman

who could wear tight blue jeans successfully, and the white T-shirt under the suede blouson jacket emphasized the swell of her breasts. She looked so different without her glasses and with her hair cut differently. He felt the kick of desire and seriously considered looking for a hidden corner where they could make love.

She stopped and looked back and held out a hand for him to take, smiling. The wind tossed her short hair and her eyes were bright. He kissed her and they walked across the springy grass with their arms round each other.

'You look great, Marianne.'

'Thank you. I want to look good for you. You look very thoughtful, as if you're remembering something.'

'Almost remembering. It's like trying to see something through thick smoke. Very frustrating.'

★   ★   ★

It was early afternoon before they reached the outskirts of Edinburgh.

'We could bypass it,' Bannerman said. 'Maybe have a look on the way back.'

'Let's do it, Mike. I remember one of the nurses raving about it. The castle, the

79

Lawnmarket, the Royal Mile, Princes Street, the Gardens, Holyrood Palace, Arthur's Seat. I've seen it on films and on telly and it's somewhere I'd really like to see.'

'OK. But we won't see much in what's left of the afternoon.'

They booked in at a small hotel on the western fringe of the city and took the receptionist's advice and went on by taxi. By early evening they had walked the length of Princes Street and the Gardens and George Street and were looking for a place to eat in Rose Street.

Marianne recalled the typewritten list of Bannerman's haunts when he was a medical student and stopped and studied the menu beside a pub door. 'This looks good.'

Bannerman frowned, staring at the name painted on the window.

'The Chimes. I think I may have drunk in another Chimes somewhere.'

'Why do you say that?'

He grinned. 'Rings a bell.'

'I hate puns. Come on; my dogs are barking and I'm starving.'

It was a high-ceilinged pub with a long bar and framed caricatures on the walls. Marianne found a table while Bannerman went to the bar and came back with their drinks.

'You look puzzled, Mike,' she prompted.

'I think I may have been here before.'

'What makes you think that?'

'The drawings on the walls seem familiar. But I don't suppose this is the only pub with caricatures on the walls, and I'd swear I've never been in Edinburgh before. What do you want to eat?'

It was dark when they left and Rose Street was busy and noisy. They walked east. As they neared the corner with Castle Street they heard the sound of angry voices at the door of a pub and two black youths came hurriedly out, shouting and turning to make obscene gestures. One of them wore a camouflaged combat jacket and a sand-coloured beret.

Bannerman moved so fast that Marianne barely saw what happened. The black youths collapsed on the ground and then he had a tight grip on her wrist and was running with her towards the corner. Halfway down the slope toward Princes Street he hailed a taxi and pushed her inside.

'Haymarket Station!'

'Mike, what on earth . . . ?'

'Shut up!' He sounded enraged but totally in control of himself. She sat in the corner of the seat and remained silent, frightened.

At Haymarket Station they left the taxi and crossed the main road and hurried along the pavement for about a block before he flagged down another taxi and gave the name of a pub half a mile from their hotel. When they reached their room he threw himself on the bed and stared at the ceiling.

'They shouldn't be able to track us, not with us switching cabs and being dropped well away from the hotel.'

'Mike, what did you do to those men?'

He reached into his pocket and displayed a foot-long black rubber cosh and mimed swinging it twice, his mouth a thin line of hate.

'But why?'

'It's the only way to deal with them, you stupid bitch. They shoot without warning, just to hear the sound of their guns, just for the excitement. They go around with their guns loaded and cocked, just looking for someone to shoot. And not always to kill; sometimes they just blast the legs off people. You have to hit them first. If you get it wrong sometimes, hit the wrong ones, it doesn't matter: there are thousands more of the bastards.'

She watched the beads of sweat running off his temples and the rapid rise and fall of his chest and the swift movement of his eyes. He was still holding the cosh, slapping it hard against the palm of his other hand.

★　★　★

82

They left Edinburgh immediately after breakfast the following day, heading north over the Forth Road Bridge into Fife. Bannerman had lain fully dressed on top of the bed for the whole night while she dozed uncomfortably beside him. Whenever she woke and looked at him his eyes had been wide open. He had risen before seven o'clock and showered and changed and then watched television until it was time for them to pack and go down for breakfast and now he was driving at a steady seventy, pushing the car to eighty or ninety miles an hour to overtake other traffic.

'You must be tired, Mike. Shall I drive for a bit?'

'Are you scared?'

'Yes. What's the hurry?'

He was silent for a few minutes then suddenly took his foot off the accelerator and reduced the speed to a steady fifty-five.

'Marianne, I suspect I may have one of my nightmares tonight or tomorrow night. Anyway, quite soon. Don't ask me how I know, 'cos I can't tell you. I don't know myself. Usually, the nightmares are a surprise, but this time I think I know it's going to happen. It's not a major problem so far as you are concerned. Nothing to worry about. But I'll probably wake you up and I want you to know what's happening.'

'All right.'

'I'm sorry if our trip is turning out to be rather less of a quiet holiday than we'd expected.'

'Just tell me what you can, Mike.'

'I will, when I know myself. It's still a bit confused. Tell me what happened last night, in Rose Street.'

'You attacked two black youths coming out of a pub.'

'Soldiers.'

'I don't think so. One of them was wearing a beret and some kind of army camouflage jacket, but . . . '

'DPM. Disruptive Pattern Material.'

'Whatever. But they weren't soldiers, just a couple of young men, students maybe. You attacked them with a cosh.'

He had driven another two miles through the Fife countryside before he spoke again.

'I'll have to think about this.'

And half an hour later: 'Christ, I'm tired! Could you take over?'

He fell asleep instantly in the passenger seat and she drove on until she could pull into a service station car-park and get out and walk some distance away and call the Institute on her mobile and ask for Dr Grace.

'I know what happened, Marianne. We had

someone nearby and there's a report in *The Scotsman*.'

'We're being tailed? You should have told me.'

'Not tailed, really. Observed.'

'So?'

'There's no danger. No one was able to give the police a clear description. You were seen getting into a taxi but there's nothing to indicate you've been traced. Should we worry about that?'

Marianne could see Bannerman still slumped in the passenger seat of the car. 'I don't think so. We changed taxis then walked the last half-mile to the hotel. Who were the black men?'

'Engineering students. They're both still in hospital with concussion and lacerations, but they'll survive. No bones broken. What made Bannerman act that way?'

'I don't know. One moment we were walking along, laughing, at peace with the world, then the black men came out of a pub and he attacked them instantaneously, with a cosh, then grabbed me and started running. In the hotel, he was wound up to breaking point, convinced he'd done the right thing, telling me about soldiers with guns shooting people for the fun of it. I think he meant black soldiers.'

'Go on.'

Marianne checked the car again. 'He was awake all night, with the cosh in his hand, sweating, eyes open, hyperventilating. It was as if he was high on something. Then this morning he drove us about fifty or sixty miles north at very dangerous speeds and suddenly ran out of steam and went out like a light. He's still asleep in the car. Now, you tell me what I need to know. I was pretty scared last night.'

'I think it's beginning to happen, Marianne. We seem to be getting to the core of the problem. What happened last night is obviously related to what happened in Africa.'

'He thinks he's going to have one of his nightmares.'

'Watch him, Marianne. Tell us everything you see.'

'Am I safe?'

'Oh, yes. You've nothing to worry about.'

Dr Leigh watched his colleague hit the key on the speaker phone. 'That's less than accurate,' he said. 'Saying she's got nothing to worry about. He could bash her skull in or stab her through the heart. Or decapitate her. He's done that before.'

'We deal in facts, Norman, not assumptions or guesses or hypotheses. Michael Bannerman killed an estimated forty-five people just once and never did it before or since.'

'He could have killed those two youths in Edinburgh.'

'But he didn't, fortunately. Hard skulls. They'll recover.'

★ ★ ★

It was early in the evening before Bannerman woke and stretched his neck and looked across at Marianne.

'Where are we?'

'In a car-park on the front at St Andrews. I let you sleep, but I phoned and booked a room for us at a hotel. How do you feel?'

'Fine, apart from a stiff neck. Hungry.'

'We missed lunch. You're not feeling violent at all, I hope?'

'Anything but. Meek and mild.'

'Do you remember what happened in Edinburgh?'

He nodded. 'There was a problem. I dealt with it. Let's go. I need a shower and a meal.'

They signed in and showered and changed then went down to dinner and he was polite and light-hearted and amusing. They strolled through the town then returned to the hotel and he made love to her vigorously. Then they fell asleep and woke late. On a morning of high white clouds and sunshine and a cooling breeze off the sea they walked for miles through the town and along the beach and back again then over the Old Course.

'The Road Hole looks quite different from the way it does on television.'

Marianne stared up at him. 'How do you know? Do you play golf?'

'I don't know.'

He watched two old men pitch on and take three each to get down and put his hands together and watched his fingers go instinctively into the interlocking grip, the right little finger between the index and second fingers of the left hand, the thumbs down the imaginary shaft, the V between the right thumb and forefinger pointing towards his right shoulder. A good, strong grip.

So he had played golf in the past, in the time that was lost to him.

He leant against the wall and watched four groups play the 17th and drive off up the 18th towards the green in front of the clubhouse. Had he played here or were the memories just the result of watching the Open on television? And how did he know about the Open? Last year's Open had been played at Carnoustie, not St Andrews, and he could remember nothing from before then. He felt a powerful urge to have a club in his hands and a ball in front of him on the short green grass; he closed his eyes and imagined the backswing and the downswing and the crack of the clubhead hitting the ball and the follow-through and watching the ball soar and land and bounce . . .

They ate lunch in a pub then walked for a while before going back to the hotel to fall asleep on the bed, tired from the exercise and the fresh air. When he woke late in the afternoon Marianne grunted and turned over on her side and showed no sign of wakening. He plugged in the laptop and connected.

Dr Grace. We're in St Andrews, Scotland. It seems I may have played golf in the past. Yesterday we toured Edinburgh and I attacked two black soldiers. All I can say is that the mere sight of them created a terrible rage in me, which I don't understand. I feel vaguely uncertain but not regretful or guilty. They were the enemy but it was Edinburgh so I'm not sure about everything. I'll let you know if it all becomes clearer. Bannerman.

He stared at the screen for a long time then hit SEND. Then he opened the mini-bar and prepared a whisky and soda and sat at the window looking out at the old stone houses and the street and the shops and the traffic, his face troubled.

Marianne turned over on the bed and

sighed and murmured something unintelligible and went on sleeping. He studied her face, delighting in the dark lashes and the neat little nose and the shapely mouth, the clear skin with its scatter of brown freckles, the slim brown hands, the small waist and the curve of the hips.

We make love together, he thought, marvelling; *she does me the honour of being intensely intimate with me. She puts her naked body against mine with every indication of pleasure. How lucky can one loony get?*

He drank a second miniature of Grouse and soda then went to the bathroom to relieve himself. A stranger's face stared at him from the bathroom mirror. Short dark hair, grey showing above the ears. A crisp dark beard, grey appearing on the chin below the corners of the mouth. A squashed nose, the right eyebrow split by a white scar. Grey eyes, narrowed and cautious.

In his toilet bag was the electric shaver he used to tidy up the short hairs round his mouth and on his neck, and it had a trimmer attachment. It was an uncomfortable process, removing the beard then shaving the sensitive skin, and when he splashed on the aftershave it stung like hell, but there was no doubt he had made a major change in his appearance.

The skin where the beard had been was paler than the rest of his face, but a few days in the sun would take care of that.

But why? Why this urge to change his appearance? So they wouldn't be able to find him? But they knew where he was. He'd just e-mailed them.

Don't know. Maybe it's someone else I'm worried about. Black soldiers? Never mind. Trust your instincts.

When Marianne woke she stared at him in surprise. 'You look ten years younger.'

'How old do you think I am?'

'Mid-thirties, maybe.'

He touched his cheek with a fingertip. 'It hurts. It feels as if my skin is shrinking.'

'It probably is, if you've had your beard for a long time. Try this.' She massaged some skin cream into his face. 'Better?'

'Yes. How long are we booked in for?'

'Open-ended.'

'We'll move on tomorrow.'

'Where to?'

'I'm not sure. West, I think.'

'We're on the coast here,' she said. 'You said you wanted to visit the coast.'

'I think it's the wrong sea.'

5

The electrifying concussion of gunfire came without warning. The window exploded into flying shards of glass which sparkled in the sunlight as they hurtled around the room and white plaster dust burst out of the interior walls and filled the air as the bullets struck and ricocheted. Then a sweating black face under a sand-coloured beret showed momentarily in the opening and he saw an AK47 being pointed into the room by two shiny black hands. The gun jerked wildly as it was fired and the sound was deafening, robbing him of his senses. It was impossible to think clearly.

'Down!' He threw himself on the concrete floor and looked towards Karen in time to see her collapse at the end of the bench, her face red with blood.

People in the ward next door were screaming then there were more bursts of gunfire and more screaming. Then shouting and more gunfire and the thud and ricochet of bullets and the crash of breaking glass and more screaming.

The sweating black face appeared over the

windowsill, looking in, eyes wide with fear and excitement, and he heard the rattle of the Kalashnikov being reloaded and grabbed the bottle and pushed it into his shirt pocket and scuttled across the gritty concrete, trying to keep low, trying to save himself. He felt for Karen's pulse then realized the grey mess beside her head was her brain. The room darkened and when he looked up he saw the soldier filling the bright square of the window, confident now, the yellow teeth bared in the sweating face, the eyes staring, the gun pointing straight at him.

I'm going to die here. I'm going to die in a shitty, bug-ridden, under-funded hospital in the asshole of nowhere, just when I've made a major breakthrough in medical research. All that sweat and the fevers and the infections in two continents comes to this: gunned down by a black teenage bastard with a Russian gun. He doesn't know who I am and he'll never give the matter a thought. It's just not fucking right. It's all fucking wrong . . .

'Mike!'

Years of bloody work, years of the shits and rashes and slabbering cream between my toes and in my crotch and armpits and sleeping with unattractive women because there was no one else available and getting there and all of a sudden . . .

'Mike! Mike, wake up. It's all right. It's just a bad dream. Let it go.'

He felt a hand on his head and gripped the slim arm tightly and heard a gasp of pain.

'Easy, Mike. Bad dream. Come out of it. It's Marianne. No problem. Let it go. It's all over. It's just a dream.'

Sanity came instantly. He opened his eyes and saw her silhouetted against the window and knew they were in a hotel room on the east coast of Scotland. St Andrews. Mussels then venison steaks for dinner then a walk down to the shore then good sex in a big soft bed.

Maybe that's the answer. Don't have the nightmare on my own. Have someone with me to tell me it's just a dream.

He released her arm. 'Did I hurt you?'

'Just a bit.'

'I'm sorry. Don't worry about it. It's something from my past, something I don't understand. Did I frighten you?'

She found the bedside light and switched it on. She looked pale and shocked. She leant over him, the beautiful little breasts bare, the nipples soft, the dark triangle of pubic hair showing between her thighs.

'I was frightened for you.' She used the sheet to wipe his face. 'All right now?'

'Yes.'

'What frightened you?'

'Nothing. I wasn't scared. It never scares me, but I don't know why. No, wait.' He breathed deeply a few times. 'Yes, I was scared. At that stage of it. But you woke me earlier than usual, before I got angry, so I was still scared. Does that make sense? It doesn't make sense to me.'

'I don't understand. Do you want a drink?'

'Please.'

She pulled a T-shirt over her nakedness then opened the minibar and poured a stiff whisky and soda and a gin and tonic while he wiped the sweat from his face and felt his breathing ease and looked at the backs of her legs. She had superb legs, slim and shapely and smooth. Why are women always sexier half-covered than naked?

'Well, Marianne: enjoying your holiday?'

'It has its good times and its bad times.'

He shivered and forced a smile. 'I usually have the dream just every few weeks, so that should be it for the time being.'

'And you won't attack the next black man you see?'

He took the glass and swallowed half the whisky. 'That was wrong, wasn't it? Afterwards I thought I'd done the right thing but I know now it was all wrong. Christ, my mind's a mess.'

'What were you dreaming about?'

He leaned back on the pillow, feeling the familiar tremor in his muscles. 'I don't know if it's all imaginary or if it's something that happened to me that I can't remember. A black youth in a camouflage jacket shooting at me through a window. A young American woman called Karen being killed. I know the dream usually goes on a lot longer, but I can't remember the details. Maybe you shouldn't have wakened me so quickly.'

'You were in a state.'

'I'm not complaining. But it's all a lot clearer this time than ever before.'

There were goose-bumps on her arms and her knees were trembling.

'Come back to bed. I'm going to have a shower.'

When she had fallen asleep he lay on his back and stared into the darkness. He could remember more of the nightmare this time, probably because he'd been wakened out of it so abruptly. The name Karen, for a start; that was new. Previously she had just been a body on the floor, blood and brains on the concrete beside her. He still couldn't remember who she was, but she was closer now. And the bottle, whatever it was; he couldn't recall that from any other time.

Is it a film I'm remembering? Am I getting

mixed up with something I've seen at the movies or on television? Or did it really happen? Where the hell could I have been to find myself being shot at by a black soldier?

★   ★   ★

In the morning they drove west through Perth and Crieff, past Loch Earn and along Glen Dochart, then past Loch Awe and Loch Etive until they reached the sea and turned south towards Oban and parked the car and walked along the front. A couple passed eating fish and chips.

'I'm hungry,' Marianne said, sniffing. 'I want fish and chips. A place like this, fishing boats and so on, they must do a great fish supper.'

They ate sitting on a bench near the ferry terminal, looking at the assortment of small craft tied up along the pier.

'My dad has a small boat,' Marianne said. 'A day sailer. He wanders around the Norfolk Broads in it, all by himself because Mum hates getting her bum wet. He never talks about the back of the boat; it's always the stern and it's not ropes but painters and warps and sheets. He even has a little peaked cap with an anchor on it.'

She glanced at Bannerman but there was

nothing to indicate that she was stirring any memories.

'Is this the right sea, the one you're looking for?'

'Must be, I suppose. It's the only other one there is.'

'So?'

He shrugged. 'So nothing. Not yet, anyway.'

'I'll have to find a toilet. Back shortly.'

Out of sight, she called the Institute on her mobile; there was a delay while Dr Grace was traced to the restaurant and returned to her office. Marianne brought her up-to-date.

'Tell me more about his nightmare, Marianne.'

'I've told you everything. There wasn't a lot. But he said he'd remembered more than on any previous occasion, although wakening up early meant he didn't have time to reach the end. I may have made a mistake there; maybe I should just have let him continue. But I was worried about him.'

The silence was criticism in itself.

'There's some new material in what you've told me, Marianne, and he probably wouldn't have remembered if you hadn't wakened him, so it's swings and roundabouts. If it happens again, let him go on a bit longer. Suggest to him that he write a description of it in his diary. Tell him you've heard that's a good way of sorting out scrambled memories.'

'He says it probably won't happen for another couple of weeks.'

'I know. Is he still showing the urge to look for something on the coast?'

'Yes. He seemed quite certain it wasn't the east coast, but there's nothing yet to confirm it's the west coast.'

'Go with it, Marianne. Keep me informed. He isn't sending us his usual daily reports.'

'He hasn't used his laptop at all.'

'Prompt him, but carefully.'

She tucked the mobile away in an inside pocket and went in search of a toilet.

You could have asked after me, you snotty bitch.

*   *   *

Bannerman felt tired but relaxed. He sat in the passenger seat with his elbow out the window, the road map in his lap, and watched the scenery as Marianne drove north and east up Loch Linnhe and across the Ballachulish Bridge towards Fort William. Nothing seemed familiar. It was all new to him.

He glanced across. Marianne was a woman who drove in a very proper fashion, hands at ten to two on the wheel, concentrating on the road ahead, checking the mirror regularly, as if she had been formally trained. He felt safe with her.

And not just with the driving. Maybe it was something to do with her being a nurse. She seemed ready and willing to care for him, to cope with his . . . problems. She was reassuring.

She looked good. The sun had been strong while they were in St Andrews and again today and she seemed to tan easily, going brown rather than red. The slim hands on the steering wheel were especially attractive, the skin smooth and golden.

'I wish our trip could have been a little less traumatic, Marianne.'

She smiled without taking her eyes off the road. 'It'll be my turn next, Mike. You'll discover I'm shit-scared of creepy-crawlies and hate cabbage and get airsick in slightly less than four seconds. I think this is what's called the period of adjustment, when we get to know about each other. All couples go through it. Are we a couple?'

'I hope so. I'll be disappointed if we're not. I suspect it'll all depend on my getting shot of my problems, which may involve you in a bit of an uproar. Stick with me, please.'

'OK.'

After a while he said: 'I've no doubt you've noticed the absence of the word 'love' in our relationship. It's not because I haven't thought of it. Rather, it's because I'm in no position to commit myself or demand that kind of commitment. I don't want to tie you down in case it turns out I'm some kind of loony. As things stand, you can dump me any time you want. I think it has to be that way.'

'It's enough that you mentioned it. Fort William coming up, but it's still early. Where are we going?'

He studied the map. 'Through the town and then north to Invergarry then we'll go west towards the coast again.'

'Didn't you say you e-mailed your doctors every day? I haven't seen you do that.'

'Probably because we're going at it like rabbits when I should be on the laptop. I'll try to find time tonight. I'm supposed to keep a diary as well, but I haven't done that either. What's to say? 'Drove, ate, bonked. Drove, ate, bonked.' It's a dull life.'

She laughed and waited a few seconds before saying: 'Maybe you should try describing your nightmare in your diary. It might help you to, I don't know, exorcise it, perhaps.'

'Perhaps.'

Elliot Pryce read the e-mail from the doctors and picked up the phone and was vaguely annoyed that Dr Grace was still in her office long after normal working hours. It would have been satisfying to invade her privacy at home.

'Is this all you have?'

'What we have is a lot more than we had yesterday, Mr Pryce. Bannerman's nightmare has always been the prime source of information, but so far we haven't been able to get into it. Now we've made an entry. He remembers the beginning of the attack on the hospital.'

'So?'

'So now we hope for more.'

'And? Christ, is that it!'

'You're missing the point, Mr Pryce. He remembers it. With luck he'll go on to remember what happened next. Which is what the Executive wants.'

'It's what I want, Doctor.'

'On behalf of the Executive, I think you said.'

'Don't even think of trying to go over my head, Doctor. Don't even think of it. That is esoteric territory where amateurs get badly burnt.'

'Wouldn't dream of it, Mr Pryce. I'll keep you informed.'

Pryce replaced the phone and wished Dr Grace an early and painful death. *I'm losing her*, he thought. *She knows she has a value. I'll have to bring her into line. I'll have to give her a fright.*

* * *

They drove through the long northern twilight, Bannerman at the wheel.

'Does it never get dark up here?' Marianne asked.

'It will soon. We'd better find a hotel.'

They found a room in Kyle of Lochalsh in time for a bar supper and ate looking out at the new bridge across the islands to Skye.

'You seem to have recovered from your nightmare,' Marianne said. 'Do you feel all right?'

'Fine,' Bannerman said. 'The nightmare is a bit of a strain at the time but the effects don't last. Look, I'm anxious not to scare you. I don't want you thinking I'm some kind of loony. I don't want you thinking you may be in danger. It's not like that.'

'I worry about you, not myself.'

'Don't. I've had this problem for ages and it hasn't blown my mind. It's just something that comes and goes.'

'No more sudden acts of violence?'

Bannerman studied his fingers, stroking a white scar which ran up the back of his left hand and vanished under his watch. Probably from the accident.

'I won't lie to you, Marianne. There's a lot I don't remember. The memories are trapped inside my head and I think they're beginning to come back, but it looks like being a painful process. I'll understand if you prefer not to get involved.'

'I am involved.'

'I don't know what sort of person I am. I may be a nice guy or a real bastard. I may have the kind of past you read about in the papers, or maybe not.'

Marianne sipped her wine and made a show of relaxing in the chair. 'Right now you're acting from instinct instead of memory and you're making a pretty good job of it. That's enough for me. I think everyone's true character is a matter of instinct and, forgetting the odd burst of GBH, I like your character.'

'You can walk away any time you want.'

She nodded. 'I will if I have to.'

He smiled at her eyes. 'Do you want to go for a walk or do you want to go for a walk and then make love?'

'Yes.'
'Unanimous.'

★   ★   ★

Later, when they had made love slowly and completely, they sat naked in the window seat and drank instant coffee and ate biscuits and looked out at the sea swirling under the bridge.

'Where are we going tomorrow, Mike? Any ideas?'

'None at all. Except that I feel I'm getting close to whatever it is I'm looking for. Don't ask me how I know, because nothing I've seen means anything to me; it's just a feeling. When the major part of your life is a black hole you have no memories to rely on so you learn to trust your instincts and I have an instinct about . . . a stretch of coastline. Sea and rocks and short grass. Small white flowers. Dried seaweed in a long line. Stones that are shiny when wet. Cold water, so cold it hurts when you stand in it. A huge sky full of white clouds riding on a strong wind. A little white house. Sheep on the road.'

She saw that his eyes were closed and his hands moving as he remembered.

'Electricity on poles. Rusty cars. A narrow road. Kittens in a ditch. Black and white collies. A wooden shed full of peat.'

She waited, intent, but he seemed almost asleep.

'An old clinker-built boat beside the house with a man burning off the paint. Blue paint.'

He rose suddenly and went into the bathroom and the door banged shut. When he returned ten minutes later he got into bed and pulled the covers over his head and turned his back on her.

* * *

Over breakfast Bannerman was quiet but not uptight. Marianne restricted the conversation to the essentials. When they went out to the car and tossed their bags into the back seat he got into the driving seat and studied the map.

'We'll stick to the coast as much as possible. It looks as if the road will be pretty narrow, but I don't suppose it'll be too busy.'

'Fine.'

They went north through Sheildaig and Torridon and turned left at Kinlochewe and ran up the south-west shore of Loch Maree. The blue skies and sunshine of the previous day persisted and the views were breathtaking.

'There's supposed to be a monster in

there,' Bannerman said, nodding towards the dark water. 'Like in Loch Ness.'

'Where did you learn that?'

He thought for a long time before answering. 'I don't know.'

When they reached Gairloch he took the right fork.

'Why not go left?' Marianne said, 'it seems to follow the coast.'

'Dead end.'

'How do you know?'

'I must have seen it on the map.' But he frowned, puzzled.

Later, as they approached Aultbea, he stopped in a lay-by and they looked down at Loch Ewe and the Isle of Ewe.

'Loch Ewe is where the Russian convoys assembled during the war,' he said. 'I read a book about it.'

'Is that making you think of something?'

He was silent for a long time. 'I get the impression there's some significance to what I'm looking at, but God knows what.'

Later, Marianne looked up from the map and pointed. 'That's Gruinard Island. Isn't that where the Government carried out experiments with anthrax or something equally nasty during the war? No one was allowed to land there for years afterwards. Maybe not yet, for all I know.'

'That's the place, yes. I read somewhere that . . . '

She braced herself hurriedly as he braked hard enough to send blue smoke drifting out from under the car. Then he drove on another hundred yards and pulled into a lay-by and switched off the engine.

'What, Mike?'

'It's an island I'm looking for!'

'Which island?'

'Hell, I don't know.'

'And how do you know?'

He shook his head. 'That's a hard one to answer.' He exhaled noisily. 'You must have seen those irritating bits on the telly where some over-enthusiastic editor has cut the film into half-second fragments — a stream of images on screen just long enough for you to recognize something but not verbalize. That's what my mind is like at times. Other times I get the equivalent of a single still photograph which just won't go away. I have to try to make sense of all this. I'm forced to make assumptions, connect things, interpret, extrapolate. It's not easy. I can't trust any conclusion I reach so I tend not to act on those conclusions. But I think I'm looking for an island.'

Marianne spread the map across their knees.

'How many islands do you need? There are hundreds. The west coast of Scotland is nothing but islands. Can't you remember a name?'

Bannerman shook his head. She read the expression on his face and took his hand and squeezed it.

'Don't get depressed, Mike. You're making progress. It won't all come back at once.'

'You sound like my doctors.'

Careful, she thought. *He mustn't make that connection.*

'I'm not really qualified to give you advice, Mike. I'm a nurse, OK, but all I can do is try to encourage you.'

'You're doing a great job, Marianne. I need you and I'm very glad you're here and I'm constantly amazed at your tolerance. I'll make it up to you, somehow.' He smiled and leaned over to kiss her. 'How would it be if I took you up on to the moor somewhere and made love to you with the skylarks overhead and the heather tickling your bare bum and the sheep standing around muttering to each other in the Gaelic and looking Calvinistically scandalized?'

'Do sheep mutter? I'd like to hear that.'

They found a place a few miles down the road, among some birch trees, and made love swiftly and passionately.

'You promised me tickly heather and skylarks and all I got was damp grass and a seagull. And the sheep were giggling. In the Gaelic.'

'We may have been in the wrong place. We'll try again another time.'

'Promises, promises.' She ran her fingers through his hair and pulled him down and kissed him. 'Anywhere you want it, lover. You have a knack of creating considerable excitement in a small Essex person.'

★   ★   ★

'This will have to be quick. Bannerman's in the shower. He thinks he's looking for an island. Does that mean anything to you?'

'Yes, but we want him to find it for himself, Marianne. That's vital.'

'There are thousands of the bloody things! Give me a hint so I can edge him in the right direction.'

The silence seemed to last an age. The water hissed in the bathroom. She could hear muffled voices as Dr Grace consulted someone.

'Rousay in Orkney.'

'Spell that, please.'

They ate dinner then went for a walk through the village in the gathering darkness.

'Gloaming,' Bannerman said. 'That's what twilight is called in Scotland. Gloaming. It sounds right.'

'It's very romantic, whatever it is. It's easy to imagine impressionable young lassies getting inquisitive about what men have under their kilts on an evening like this.'

'Midge bites, probably.' Bannerman said. 'Let's get back to the hotel. I remember . . . '

'What?'

'Bites.'

'Is that all?'

'Yes. Something about insect bites. Having to apply antiseptic immediately. Have I spoiled the moment?'

'Effectively, yes, but we'll recover. I was thinking, if we don't know which island you're looking for, could we go to Orkney? We could be there tomorrow afternoon, and it's a place I've always wanted to see and never thought I would. I was quite into George Mackay Brown for a while.'

'Is this a former lover?'

'No! He's a writer who lived in Orkney. Novels and poems. 'Islands like sleeping whales'. I'd love to go there.'

'Is that where they have all those Stone Age houses and tombs?'

'That's the place, yes.'

'Seduce me and I'll take you there.'

'Starting now?'

'I think we should wait till we get back to our room. It would make it easier to climb the stairs.'

'You still haven't done your diary or e-mailed your doctors.'

'Tomorrow morning, before we leave.'

★   ★   ★

Angela Grace woke just after she had fallen asleep and listened to the phone ringing beside her bed and knew it was Elliot Pryce and hated him more than she had hated anyone in her life, even counting George, who had made losing her virginity such a ghastly experience that she had never been to bed with a man since.

'Yes?'

'Why Orkney?'

'Because that's where his father lives.'

'You knew this?'

'Of course.'

'Then why the fuck didn't you just put Bannerman in a car or a helicopter and take him up there instead of all this farting about, for fuck's sake?'

Dr Grace had drunk three large glasses of wine after getting home and she was tired and offended by his language and by this intrusion into her privacy and wanted to lie back on the pillow and go to sleep.

'Because this is the way it has to be done. We're dealing with a human mind, not a page of bloody figures. Bannerman is fragile. Do it your way and he'll finish up in a padded cell and you'll lose everything. Do it my way and we'll unpick his brain and take out everything we want. Your choice.'

'I'm going to have to report to the Executive that I have doubts about your competence, Doctor.'

'If you bring in someone new you'll set the programme back a good eight months, Mr Pryce. A point I shall be happy to explain to the Executive. So fuck off.'

Elliot Pryce slammed down the phone and lay back in bed. Shirley rolled over and pushed her breasts against him.

'Piss off, you fat slut!'

'Charming, I'm sure. Having a bit of trouble, are we? Need a bit of coaxing?'

'Please. Did you keep your knickers on?'

'Of course. They're not too clean.'

'Good.'

'Quite smelly, really.'

'You haven't wet them, have you?'

'I think I may have.'

'That's terrible.'

He rolled on to his back and waited for her

and tried desperately to forget about Michael Bannerman and Dr Angela Grace and Dr Norman Leigh and the bloody technicians with their screens and keyboards and hidden cameras and the claustrophobic basement and what he was going to have to say to the Executive. He had to convince them that everything was going well and that a result was pending and that the mounting bill was justified and the bastards were running out of patience and if the Bannerman problem wasn't solved very soon he was going to find himself managing a small fertilizer factory in a tropical country where the heat and the humidity would aggravate his skin problem.

'Is that nice?'

It was difficult to speak.

6

Bannerman rose early and worked at the laptop while Marianne showered and dressed and made coffee for them. He went into his diary first and struggled to write an account of his nightmare but it was hard work.

Marianne took his empty cup. 'I'll go down and find out about ferries to Orkney. I'll wait for you.'

He finished without checking the spelling and grammar, relieved that it was over but knowing he would go back to it; there was more he could say. It was as if each sentence, each remembered image, reminded him of more. Oddly, there was a certain catharsis about the exercise, as if writing about his nightmare were getting rid of it, as if he were downloading it from his mind to the computer to free up memory space in his head.

He showered and dressed and sat down again.

Dr Grace. Just spent the night in Scourie, which is somewhere on the wild north-west coast of Scotland, not far from the top left hand corner. Sorry about the gap in reporting to you. I've had one of my nightmares, but this time Marianne woke me and I remembered some of it. I've written an account in my diary and you'll see it when I get back. The urge to find somewhere on the coast has come to a bit of a dead end because I think what is nagging at me is an island and there are hundreds of them around here. So I'm stuck, unless something comes back to me. Marianne wants to visit Orkney, which is just up the road a bit, so we're going there then I expect we'll make our way back. Bannerman.

He sent then stood at the window looking out at the shore and the sea. Today the sky was grey and the wind was getting up. A day for travelling.

When he went downstairs Marianne came out of the phone booth carrying a brochure.

'There are two ferries from Scrabster to Orkney, but we might not make the noon sailing so I've booked us in for the one at five o'clock, so there's no rush, although we should be there an hour early.'

'Well done. Ready for another Scottish hotel breakfast?'

'Loins girded, belt loosened. Do women have loins?'

'You do and they're the most important thing in my life right now. You look great.

116

You've changed colour. You're a lovely shade of coffee.'

'You're looking rather toothsome yourself, big boy. I think you needed a holiday.'

She's actually very beautiful, Bannerman thought, surprised. *I've noticed men glancing at her. Hell, I can't take my eyes off her myself.*

★   ★   ★

'Promising,' Dr Grace said when she had read Bannerman's e-mail. 'There are definite signs of progress. Should we ask him to send his diary?'

'It might inhibit him,' Dr Leigh said. 'He'll be back in a few days. Let's wait till then. I've a feeling we may have reached some kind of watershed and I think we should let him run with it, if that's what you do with watersheds.'

'You may be right.'

Norman Leigh opened the file on his desk. 'We know very little about his father. Two very routine pages. One photograph taken in 1976. Nothing to explain the upset in the family.'

'I don't suppose it seemed relevant at the time,' Dr Grace said. 'But I agree, it's a pity we don't know more; we have no way of guessing in advance what's likely to happen if they meet. When you think about it, we don't even know if his father is still alive. Check on that.'

Don't give me orders, you dried-up old prune!

He used the Internet to check the Orkney phone book. 'He's still listed.'

'Good. I was nervous about releasing Bannerman into the community; now I'm scared rigid because he's away in Scotland, out of our control.'

'It may be what he needs. A bit of freedom.'

'I had Elliot Pryce on the phone again last night, Norman. Swearing at me. Questioning our competence. Making threats. We're going to have to give him something concrete very soon. I swore at him.'

'Good for you, Angela. That'll teach him.'

I may get the bloody woman's job yet.

★   ★   ★

They sat on a bench on the upper deck of the roll-on, roll-off ferry *St Ola*, feeling the chill of the sea wind penetrating their clothing, watching the clouds breaking up. The Pentland Firth was lively but neither of them was prone to seasickness.

'You're very quiet, Mike.'

118

'Not really. Just taking in a host of new sights and sounds and wondering what they mean to me, if anything.'

'Have you considered the possibility that your mystery island may be here in Orkney? I was looking at a map on the wall near the purser's office and Orkney is all islands.'

'Show me.'

They staggered downstairs and he stared at the composite Ordnance Survey 1/50,000 map for a long time then shrugged.

'Nothing. Let's have a drink.'

Towards the end of the two-hour crossing they went back on deck and watched the towering cliffs of Hoy slide past off the starboard side and then the town of Stromness appear to port as the ship slowed and manoeuvred and eventually berthed neatly at the pier. They went down to the car deck and waited to be directed off the ship and into the town.

'There's a hotel a few miles out,' Marianne said. 'The Standing Stones. We could try there.'

They were able to get a room and after dinner they went out and walked along the shore of the Loch of Stenness. The sky was still bright, the overcast clearing, and the wind had dropped to a whisper.

'Listen,' Bannerman said, stopping.

'What?'

'Silence.'

She listened and smiled. 'It's incredibly quiet.' She moved on but Bannerman remained where he was, his face raised to the sunset, as if he were smelling the air.

'Like this,' he murmured. 'It's like this.'

'What is, Mike?'

'The place I'm looking for. It's quiet like this. Quieter. Nothing moves except the sea.'

'Where is it, love?'

He shook his head. 'I don't know. But it's important to me, somehow. I must find it.'

★　★　★

In the morning they went a mile up the road and made their stooped way through the tunnel into the heart of the burial mound of Maes Howe and marvelled at the sophistication of the construction; nearby were the standing stones of Stenness and over the bridge between the Loch of Stenness and the Loch of Harray was the giant Ring of Brodgar. They walked round the circle of standing stones then lay on the grass on top of a mound and rested. Today there were skylarks but there were also other visitors and they were constrained to quick kiss. They drove on to the visitor centre at Skara Brae and bought an OS map of Orkney Mainland, then took the conducted tour of the 4,500-year-old village, then walked along the beach, arms round each other.

'We'll have to buy jerseys,' Bannerman said. 'This place is incredible, but you have to be well wrapped up.'

'I spoke to a woman in the hotel and she said Orkney knitwear is gorgeous,' Marianne said. 'Not cheap, but gorgeous. All hand-knitted. Kirkwall is the place to go for it.'

'We'll go to Kirkwall.'

They spent the rest of the day in Kirkwall, eating crab salads then buying two huge and intricately-patterned jerseys and going round the cathedral and the town before driving back to the hotel to sit in the bar, tired by their exertions.

'I wouldn't mind a sleep before dinner,' Marianne said. 'And I mean a sleep. It's not a euphemism for nooky.'

'Sounds good. I could shoot off an e-mail then join you.'

'Let's do that.'

She lay on the bed and pretended to be asleep while he worked at the laptop. When he lay down beside her she turned to him and relaxed and when he woke her it was time to go down for dinner. Over the seafood starter she sipped her wine and said: 'Mike, maybe you should look through the phone book in case you have any relatives here. Maybe this is where your island is. Do you know anything about your family?'

'I'm not even sure my name is Michael Bannerman. It's all a bit of a mystery. I was pulled out of a wrecked car, the driver was dead, I had nothing on me but a watch with that name engraved on the back. The people at the Institute say they've made all sorts of enquiries but can't find out anything about me. And I keep forgetting my name, as if it weren't really mine.'

'Waste of time, maybe, trying the phone book.' She had already looked; the answer was there, but he had to find it for himself. 'What do you want to do tomorrow?'

'We'll have a look at the brochures in the lobby.'

Over coffee in the lounge they went through a selection of leaflets; there was far more to see than they could possibly manage in a few days. Marianne watched him glance from one brochure to the next and saw him discard the one for Rousay and wondered how she was going to direct him in that direction. Perhaps a straightforward expression of interest in the island, although that seemed a bit obvious . . .

She saw him frown and go back to the

Rousay brochure and stare at it. He rose. 'Back in a moment.'

She could see him through the glass doors of the lounge. He went to the phone in the lobby and searched through the book and stood there for a long time before coming back to spread the OS map across the table.

'I fancy Rousay,' he said. 'A nice little trip on a ferry then we could drive round the island and have a look at Midhowe Cairn and Midhowe Broch and there's a hotel where we could have lunch. And there are more tombs and Viking houses than you could shake a stick at.'

When they went to bed he seemed restless and preoccupied and lay for a time with the light on, studying the map. She slipped an arm round his waist and lay against him, pressing her breasts against his back and her thighs against his.

I'm beginning to feel like some kind of traitor. They're paying me very well to do this job and the sex is great and I'm seeing places I've never seen before and if I can help them get into his mind I'll be flavour of the month with Spire Matte Interco. But I'm beginning to feel like some kind of traitor. No, that's not the word. Bitch, maybe. Or prostitute.

Bannerman switched off the light and

turned to her. 'Not too tired by all your exertions?'

'One more exertion.'

'You don't have to.'

'I want to.' She found his face in the darkness and pulled him into a long kiss and arched her back as he caressed her spine. She slipped her thigh between his and moved against him and felt his reaction. 'There now: you're not as tired as you thought you were.'

'You could rouse Tutankhamun.'

'There's more. Hold on to your crown, Great Pharaoh.'

★　★　★

The Tingwall ferry was a small platform capable of taking six cars, with the engine room and bridge forward. Bannerman followed a van down the ramp and clattered over the metal plates on to the deck. They stood at the rail and watched the other vehicles come aboard and heard the engine rumble as the boat moved away from the pier. The morning mist had cleared and the sun sparkled on the water and there was a hint of warmth in the wind.

'I love this,' Marianne said, slipping her hand into his; he had been silent during the drive across Mainland from the hotel. 'It's invigorating. There's a marvellous feeling about taking a small ferry to an island. Do you feel it, Mike?'

He nodded and smiled at her, but she knew she did not have his full attention.

She pointed. 'Is that Rousay?'

'Must be.' He took the map from his pocket and compared it with what they could see. 'Rousay, Wyre, Gairsay, Shapinsay. I think that's Egilsay beyond Wyre, there. In a minute we should be able to see Eynhallow.'

It was a twenty minute run to the pier on Rousay.

'You drive,' Bannerman said, 'I want to look at things.'

She drove off the ferry and up the narrow road. 'Does it matter which way?'

'Go right. The road runs round the island in a circle, so it doesn't matter much which way we go.'

They stopped halfway, on the northern side of the island, and looked down a steep hill to a rocky beach and across the sea towards Westray and Eday. She noticed that he kept looking west towards a low-lying headland and a scatter of white houses. She had checked the phone book and the OS map and knew that the only Bannerman on Rousay lived in a house called Bister on Saviskaill Head. Which was where he was looking.

They drove on until they reached a T-junction at the tiny Loch of Wasbister. The main road continued left and the road going right went towards Saviskaill Head.

'Go right.' There was tension in his voice. She obeyed, saying nothing. He studied the map and the land intently. There was a final track leading off to the left and then the road deteriorated suddenly and they saw the word BISTER hand-painted on a stone.

'Stop!'

She braked. 'Where are we, Mike?'

'I think we've taken a wrong turning somewhere.'

'On an island with one road going in a circle?' She looked towards the roof and the white walls showing over a rise. 'Does this place mean something to you?'

He sighed. 'I checked the phone book. The only Bannerman on Rousay lives here. But Bister is a very common name in Orkney; it just means farm. We could be in the wrong place.'

'You're nervous.'

He nodded slowly. 'I'm not sure if I'm scared of this place being important, or if I'm scared of it not meaning anything to me. And I never came looking for people, just a place. I'm not ready for people.'

They sat in silence for a few minutes, the

engine ticking over, then Marianne said: 'If you don't go on now you'll just have to come back another time.'

'I know. All right, let's do it.'

The car swayed and jolted the half-mile to the single-storey white house with its roof of sandstone slabs. There were two stone outbuildings and a tumbledown stone wall enclosing an untended garden. Nothing moved.

'I don't see a car anywhere,' Marianne said, switching off the engine. She opened the door and got out and looked back in. 'Come on. No one's going to bite you.'

Bannerman walked across the grass to the gate in the stone wall and looked around. The sea filled the horizon to north and east; the rocky shore was just a few yards away; there were small white flowers along the base of the dyke. Marianne watched his face.

'What do you feel, Mike?'

He shrugged. 'Anticlimax. No sudden revelations. I'll see if there's anyone in.' He strode across the stony parking area beside the house and knocked firmly on the back door and waited and knocked again. When there was no reply he glanced into one of the outhouses and went to the dyke and looked over at the rocks along the shore then came back.

'Nothing.'

'You could phone later.'

'Yes, I could do that. Let's go.'

They had driven about four miles without speaking when he said: 'Stop here.

She pulled into a lay-by and switched off. 'What are you seeing?'

'Down there. Midhowe Cairn and Midhowe Broch. We've come all this way, so let's have a look at them.'

It was a long walk down the hill over the fields to the broch and the burial cairn protected by a modern building. She followed him in silence as he explored the sites.

'They call it the Ship of the Dead,' he whispered, looking down from the gantry at the exposed tomb.

'Memories?'

'There's something.' He shook his head impatiently. 'I feel like I've been here before, but I can't get hold of anything definite. The rocks below the broch seemed to mean something.'

'Don't push it, Mike. Just keep your mind open.'

The hotel was a few miles on. They parked beside a Land Rover so old the paint had faded and went into a tiny bar where the only customers were an elderly couple sitting on a bench, a black and white dog at their feet.

There was no one behind the bar.

'I'll drive back,' Bannerman said, 'so you can have a drink. Gin?'

'Please. Is there a menu?'

'Michael?'

They both looked at the old man in the corner. His grey beard hid half his face and a tweed cap covered his hair. He looked pale. The woman reached for his hand and gripped it protectively, her face nervous.

'Sorry?'

'Are you Michael Bannerman?'

'Yes. Should I know you?'

The old man exhaled slowly, his eyes riveted on Bannerman's face.

'Have you really forgotten me, Michael? Or are you still trying to hurt me?'

Bannerman stared at him, the hairs prickling at the back of his neck.

'I was in an accident. I've forgotten everything. Can you tell me who you are, please?'

'My name's Stewart Bannerman, Michael. I'm your father.'

Bannerman stared at him for a long moment then groped for a stool and sat down, his back to Marianne. The dog got to its feet and put its head between his legs and sniffed and he stroked the silky hair of its ears.

'Do you live at Bister, up at the top of the island?'

'Yes.'

'We've just been there, looking for you. Except I didn't know it was you. It was just the name. Some kind of instinct.'

'Have you really lost your memory?' The old man's voice was educated, precise, gentle. The grey eyes were direct, the mouth firm.

Was my nose like that, before it was squashed? It's a good, straight nose.

'Yes. I was in a car accident eight months ago and I suffered severe amnesia. Things are coming back, but they don't always make sense.'

'And you came here looking for me?'

A woman appeared behind the bar. 'Sorry, everyone. Busy with the menu. What can I get you?'

Marianne rose hurriedly and went to the bar. Bannerman moved from the stool he was on to one at the old man's table and studied his face.

Is this what I'll be like when I'm old? Deep lines round the eyes, bushy eyebrows, a smooth forehead, big brown hands. I won't complain.

He looked at the woman. Dark hair going grey, plump, full-mouthed, laugh-lines round the dark eyes.

'Are you my mother?'

'No. Sorry. I'm Andrea Lambert. Your father and I have been living together for about twenty years. But we have met, Michael. Don't you remember me?'

Bannerman shook his head. Marianne put drinks on the table and sat down hesitantly. 'Should I leave you alone for the moment?'

'No.' Bannerman introduced her. She shook hands awkwardly with Stewart Bannerman and Andrea Lambert.

'Can I get you a drink?' She accepted their refusals and held up a card. 'I have the menu.'

'You came looking for me, Michael?'

'I didn't know what I was looking for. I wasn't looking for people, if you see what I mean; I was looking for a place, I think. It's not all that clear. My mind's a bit of a mess these days.'

'And you went to the house?'

'Yes. I expected to find a blue boat. It wasn't there and nothing meant anything and I just accepted it was another bum steer. My life's a succession of bum steers these days.'

Stewart Bannerman smiled for the first time. His colour was coming back; his face was weatherbeaten.

'The boat was rotten. I tried to repair it but it was never going to be safe. I put a match to

131

it and bought a fibreglass Shetlander. It's moored in the loch. God, that was a long time ago. What can you remember, son?'

Bannerman closed his eyes tightly. *Son*. He felt a wave of emotion and tried to suppress it.

'Not much. Vague images of childhood up to an age I can't identify. Then nothing until eight months ago and even that is pretty hairy. Was I ever a doctor?'

'Yes. You followed me into the profession. Rather against your will, at the start, but then you became engrossed. Then I lost you.'

'What do you mean?'

Bannerman watched the glance his father exchanged with Andrea Lambert. She had plump white hands, neat fingers, compassionate eyes. They seemed able to communicate without words.

'Do you remember your mother, Mike?'

'No.'

'Nothing at all?'

'Nothing.'

Stewart Bannerman smiled wryly. 'Which leaves the way open for me to load things in my favour, but I won't. I'll try to give you a balanced picture. Drink up and we'll go home and have lunch and talk in peace. This is hardly the place for family revelations.'

Marianne drove as they followed the ancient Land Rover back along the road towards Bister. She glanced across at Bannerman, noting his look of exhaustion and the way he was slumped in his seat. It seemed better to remain silent.

'What do you think, Marianne?'

'He's your father, all right. I saw it in his face as soon as he spoke. I hadn't really looked at him till then. He's you, thirty years on.'

'What do you think he meant when he asked if I was still trying to hurt him?'

'I don't know. I think he'll tell you. I get the impression there was some kind of trauma in the family.'

'Yes, I got that impression, too.'

★ ★ ★

The door wasn't locked, Marianne thought as she followed Bannerman and Andrea Lambert into the house. Maybe they don't bother, in Orkney. The kitchen was tiny, very neat and clean.

'Go through.' the woman said. She seemed more relaxed now, in her own home. No doubt she and Bannerman's father had discussed things during the journey and reached some kind of decision about how to handle the situation.

Stewart Bannerman followed them into the small sitting room. He had removed his tweed cap to reveal a full head of grey hair and the resemblance was now much more obvious.

'Sit down, Michael. Marianne. I'll get drinks. We treat ourselves to a bar lunch a couple of times a week, but Andie will soon rustle up a meal. She's a very good cook.'

Bannerman took an armchair beside the gas fire and looked around. Two packed bookcases, a computer on a desk, amateur watercolours on the walls, a television set in a corner. Everything clean and neat and comfortable. The old man ushered Marianne into the other armchair and went to the sideboard and began to prepare drinks.

'Recognize anything, Michael?'

'Should I?'

'I think so. Things have been changed since you were here last, but I thought . . . '

'So I have been here before?'

'You lived here for a few years, from when you were about ten until you were twelve, then you had to go to high school in Kirkwall, which meant living in a hostel five days a week and coming home at weekends. It was like that until you went to university. Whisky and soda, gin and tonic: right?'

They thanked him. He took a drink to Andrea in the kitchen then sat down at the table.

'I wonder if there's any significance in the fact that we both drink whisky and soda, Michael.'

Bannerman shrugged. He still felt intensely shy. 'What happened after I went to university?'

'That, really, was the last we saw of you.'

'What do you mean?'

Stewart Bannerman stared into space and shook his head. He drank and placed the glass on the table and stared at it.

'There was always a much closer bond between you and your mother than there ever was between you and me, Michael. We were living in Helensburgh in those days. I was a surgeon in Glasgow, working all the hours God sent, and when I came home I was too tired to be much of a father. Your mother was a GP in a local practice and could spend more time with you. I don't know what went wrong. I mean, I thought everything was fine between us but I suppose it wasn't. Suddenly she wasn't there any more. She went to the States with an American doctor, leaving you and me behind. You were ten years old at the time. I suspect I overreacted a bit by getting a job here on Rousay as a GP, which was a spur-of-the-moment decision but one I've never regretted. I retired just a year ago.'

'She abandoned me?'

'Yes. She abandoned both of us.'

'She didn't try to take me with her?'

'No. Which affected you very deeply. I was a poor substitute for your mother, at least in your eyes. So far as you were concerned I had driven her away. It was a very difficult time. Then I met Andie and she came to live with me and I hoped that would give you more of a proper home life but you just saw her as someone who had come between you and your mother, which was unfair, because we didn't meet till about a year later.'

Bannerman drank and glanced at his father. 'What was she like?'

Stewart Bannerman reached out and pulled a photograph album from one of the bookcases and handed it to his son. 'She's in there.'

Bannerman turned the pages. He saw a baby and a child and a small boy and a boy in a school uniform; he saw Stewart Bannerman, beardless; he saw a woman, very beautiful, immaculately dressed, her hair in a variety of styles. She seemed very conscious of the camera. He saw himself adoring the woman.

'She abandoned me?'

'She abandoned both of us,' Stewart Bannerman said. 'You doted on her but she walked out on you. I loved her as well, but that didn't seem to matter. She needed constant proof that she was attractive and exciting, and she had a very low boredom threshold. I knew that before we married, but I thought . . . ' He shrugged.

'Where is she now?'

'I heard, not long after she went to the States, that she had moved to Canada, but with someone else. Since then, nothing.' Stewart Bannerman emptied his glass and went to the sideboard. 'You were badly affected by what happened, Michael. I was never an adequate substitute for your mother. You came back here occasionally while you were in Edinburgh but it was clearly a duty, not something you wanted to do. You worked your way through med school so you wouldn't have to accept money from me, although I sent you cash every month. I went down for your graduation and we had a ghastly meal together and today is the first time I've seen you since then.'

'I'm sorry.'

'You blamed me for the fact that your mother had left. It seemed easier to let you think that. The alternative was to let you know your mother had walked out on you which might have done serious damage.'

Stewart Bannerman distributed fresh drinks and sat down and forced a smile. 'Now tell me a little about yourself.'

'I wish I could,' Bannerman said, looking at Marianne. 'I wish I could tell you I was a credit to you, but I don't know if I ever was. When you introduced yourself you asked if I was still trying to hurt you; I wondered what you meant and now I know and I can only apologize, although it's like apologizing on someone else's behalf.'

'You're here now, Michael, which is more than I ever expected.'

★ ★ ★

They ate fried fish in breadcrumbs and new potatoes and peas with a home-made tartare sauce, then Andrea made coffee and they took turns at breaking the silence.

'What's it like here in winter?' Marianne asked.

'Dark,' Andrea said. 'A brief outbreak of daylight around noon. But not too cold. Windy, though; the wind can blow at about fifty miles an hour for three weeks at a time.'

'We make up for it in summer,' Stewart Bannerman said. 'The simmer dim: an hour

138

of twilight between sunset and sunrise.'

'Can I have another look at that photograph album?' Bannerman said.

* * *

Late in the afternoon they all walked out to the car.

'Will you come back, Michael?' Stewart Bannerman asked. 'There's the spare room. We could clear out the junk and get a double bed.'

'Yes. I want to. And we'll keep in touch by e-mail.'

'Good. Let me know how you get on with recovering your memory. Any questions, I'll answer them.'

They shook hands tentatively.

'I'm not ready yet to start calling you Dad,' Bannerman said. 'That'll take a bit longer.'

'You never called me that much even when you were a boy, Michael.'

'You make me sound like a right little shit.'

'You were never that, son. You were a lonely little boy, intelligent and sensitive, who'd been badly hurt and reacted by bottling it up. You were old beyond your years. You asked for nothing. You were self-contained and independent and I could never get close to you. We've talked more today than we ever did.'

Bannerman saw the tears in his father's eyes and instinctively reached out and touched the old man's arm.

'See you soon, Dad.'

'OK, son.'

7

Now the man burning the blue paint off the boat had a face, a brown face with a dark beard and grey eyes. The boat was supported on half a dozen old car tyres and stood on the grass beside one of the stone outbuildings. Blackened curls of paint littered the short grass and the smell of burning paraffin from the blowlamp was distinct in the clean air off the sea. The man looked up and smiled.

'Want to give me a hand, Michael?'

'I'm busy.'

Bannerman lay on his back on the bed and clenched his eyes shut in shame and regret.

I wanted to hurt him. I always wanted to hurt him. He was trying to build a bridge between us and I was determined to destroy that bridge.

It had to be about three o'clock in the morning by now; outside, it was full daylight and had been for a long time. Dawn came early in Orkney in June. There was nothing that could properly be called darkness.

Marianne moved a leg and breathed noisily in her sleep.

He saw a sudden image of his hands

carrying a fish into the kitchen and putting it in the sink and his father smiling and congratulating him. He could not hear his own reply but the sudden hurt in his father's face was obvious.

I'm sorry, Dad.

He searched his mind for more memories but nothing came except an impression of self-pity and loneliness and isolation. He felt the need to unburden himself and rose quietly and opened the laptop and connected.

Dr Grace. Still in Orkney, but leaving in the morning early, probably home tomorrow. I've found my father, living on the island of Rousay with a very nice lady called Andrea. It seems my mother abandoned me when I was a child and I reacted by blaming my father, quite unjustly. I like to think we've sorted out our differences. I'll come back some time soon and try to get to know him. That nagging memory was of the shore beside my dad's house. He and I went for a walk along the beach and he showed me where we used to fish and where he burnt a boat I remember him working on and things are a bit clearer now. Scraps of memory have become connected and I know where I fit into them. It's all a bit of a strain but I think I'm learning to handle it. Bannerman.

* * *

They managed to catch the eight o'clock ferry and had breakfast on board. Marianne brought the tray to their table and sat down and glanced at Bannerman's face. They had said very little since leaving Rousay and they had gone to bed separately, knowing it was not a time for sex.

'How are you feeling, Mike?'

'Mixed up. Sorry to be such poor company. I've had a lot to think about.'

'I know. It must be quite a shock, finding a father you didn't know you had.'

He nodded and stirred his coffee. 'It would have been good to find a father and mother and discover I had a solid home life I could return to, but it turns out my mother abandoned me and I hated my father. I can't help thinking it would have been better if I'd never found out.'

'He struck me as being a good man, Mike. Unhappy about you, but now you have the chance to do something about that. I think you should work at becoming father and son again.'

'I wish we could have stayed the night. I wish we hadn't left when we did. Do you think he understood that I don't hate him any longer?'

'I think he knew.'

'But what if I get my memory back and discover I still hate him?'

'There's such a thing as free will, Mike. You'll be able to change your feelings. Have you remembered anything more? Has being on Rousay reminded you of anything?'

'Yes. Scenes. Short sequences of very clear images. I've had some of them before, but now I understand what I'm seeing. Previously, they didn't mean anything. Now the images seem to come complete with emotions, which is new. And a bit off-putting. I can't help feeling I must have been hell to live with.'

'Maybe you're remembering the excessive emotions of a teenager. Puberty and all that. No one's completely sane at that age.'

He grinned suddenly, as if relieved that he had been given a good excuse for his behaviour. 'Good point, Marianne. Hadn't thought of that. I'll mention it to Dad.'

They drove south, stopping at the same hotel below Bamburgh Castle for the night before continuing the following day. They were back at the flats by late afternoon. They paused on the landing outside Bannerman's door.

'It would be good if you just moved in with me, Marianne.'

She dropped her bags and leant back against the banister. 'It seems a natural progression, yes, but it leaves Liz paying for the flat on her own.'

'You could share the rent till she makes some kind of arrangement and still live with me. And you wouldn't have to pay at all if you lived with me; the Institute owns the flat.'

She nodded and smiled. 'It all sounds very sensible. Open the door, lover. I'm desperate for a pee.'

* * *

There was a flurry of activity, the carrying of bags and books and clothes downstairs from the third floor to the second floor. Later in the evening, when Liz came home, they all went out for a curry.

'Janey Wainwright is looking for a place,' Liz said. 'I'll speak to her tomorrow. She'll probably want to move in immediately. Tell me about your holiday.'

Bannerman concentrated on the food and let Marianne tell the tale. 'It's magic up there, Liz. You've got to go. Wait till you see the photographs. It's so quiet and empty and peaceful and beautiful. There's only one set of traffic lights in the whole of Orkney, in the middle of Kirkwall, and everyone drives around at about forty miles an hour and is terribly polite about passing places and so on. I loved it. I didn't want to come back. When you've been in Orkney you realize London is not a civilized place.'

She glanced at Bannerman and froze. He was groping in the dish with his bare hands, finding pieces of chicken and stuffing them into his mouth. Sauce ran off his chin on to his shirt. He seized the nan bread and bit into it and chewed noisily, his eyes glaring and suspicious. When there was no chicken left he plunged the nan bread into the sauce and pushed it into his mouth, holding it with both hands, his sleeves and cuffs stained. Then he jumped to his feet and ran to the door, shouldering a waiter violently aside, and vanished into the night.

★　★　★

'Dr Grace? It's Marianne. We're back. Bannerman and Liz and I went out for a meal and he went haywire. He started eating like an animal, or at least like someone who's starving and is scared he's going to have his food stolen. Then he took off, literally ran out of the restaurant, knocking people down, still carrying the nan bread. He looked — out of

146

it. He was somewhere else. It was really scary.'

'Where are you now?'

'Liz and I are on our way back to the flats.'

'Wait. Give me time to get down to the basement.'

Marianne hurried along the pavement, the mobile pressed to her ear, Liz beside her. She heard a crackle then Dr Grace came back on.

'He's not in his flat. He's not showing on the screens.'

'What do you want me to do?'

'Be there in case he comes back. Get Liz to search the streets. I'll rouse everyone I can. Now tell me what happened in Orkney. The last thing we have is an e-mail from him, yesterday, saying he'd found his father. Did anything else happen which might have prompted this behaviour?'

* * *

Cover. I need cover, even though it's dark now. They have helicopters, so I should be under the trees. They may have heat-sensing gear, but the bastards probably won't know how to use it. That way. But don't run — walk. A running man is a man running away and is automatically a target. They'll shoot without thinking. They always do.

He crossed the street and hurried along the park railings in the deep shadow under the trees. When he found an overhanging branch he checked all around then leapt up and gripped it and swung his feet on to the top of the railings, between the spikes, and jumped into the darkness on the other side. Branches whipped his face and hands and he felt the pain from the bullet wounds in his side and leg but that was not a problem.

Make some distance. They don't like leaving the roads because the rebels are supposed to be strong in the back country. Stay in the forest, under cover. Head north-west, towards the river, then follow it down-stream and across the border. Eighty miles. Poor bloody Karen. She didn't deserve to die, like that or any other way. She was trying to help these people and they killed her.

He felt the rage. It seemed to flow through his body like fire in his veins, like raw power in his muscles.

How many did I kill? Forty-five of the bastards, but not enough. Go back, get some more? Fuck them.

He took the knife from his pocket and the blade snapped out and he moved through the trees, eyes and ears primed for any hint of them, smelling the humid African night.

★ ★ ★

They had set up a temporary base in a Transit van parked opposite Bannerman's flat. It was cramped and unsatisfactory but the best they could do at short notice. Dr Grace used her mobile to contact Marianne Shannon.

'He's not hiding in the flat, Doctor, and I've also checked the flat upstairs. There's nothing to indicate he came back here then left again. I think I'd be able to smell the curry.'

'Was he carrying his weapons?'

'I don't see them here.'

'Thank you. Stay there, Marianne. I'll let you know if he appears and if he looks dangerous we'll intercept him.'

'What's happening?'

'We have Dr Leigh and four technicians touring the area in three cars. I presume Liz is still out there as well. Does she have her mobile with her?'

'Probably.'

'I'll call her. I'll get back to you.'

When Liz Parkinson answered she was out of breath. 'No sign of him. I'm working outwards in circles from the curry house but I've seen nothing at all. Shouldn't we bring in the police, Doctor?'

'That's a possibility, Liz, but I'm going to

149

give it some time. It would be an embarrassment.'

'I think he's dangerous. He looked really weird in the restaurant. And violent. He knocked a waiter arse over tip.'

Dr Grace thought of the cosh and the flick knife and felt the chill of approaching disaster.

'I don't think that's a problem, Liz. Keep in touch.' She closed the connection and her mobile rang immediately.

'Pryce. You left a message. It had better be important.'

Maybe I should start smoking, Dr Grace thought. Cigarettes or maybe an occasional reefer or whatever they're called these days. Joints. Something to give me a moment of calm when everything's going wrong.

'Bannerman seems to have had some kind of crisis in a restaurant. He behaved oddly then ran out and we're trying to find him.'

'What does this mean, Doctor?'

'It may very well be a step in the right direction. It has to mean his memory is coming back and it's inevitably going to be rather traumatic for him . . . '

'Or it could mean he's running around London with a knife and a cosh killing people. And that will mean he's out of our

150

control and therefore useless to us. Christ, if the police get hold of him we'll lose him for ever!'

'All he's done is knock over a waiter . . . '

'You don't know what he's doing right now.' He could be hacking orphans to bits!'

He's genuinely angry this time, Dr Grace thought. *This time it's not for effect and that is truly frightening.*

'What would you advise, Mr Pryce?'

'Find him. Lock him up. Drug him. Get control over him. How many people do you have searching for him?'

'Six.'

'I'll have another dozen there within half an hour. Where are you?'

She described the van and its location and the phone went dead.

'Shit!' The driver turned to look at her and she denied herself the relief of tears.

★　★　★

How far have I come? Miles. Hard to calculate. Take ten. Deal with the wounds.

He sat at the foot of a tree and pulled off his jacket and shirt and used the knife to cut the shirt into strips, then tied the strips end to end and used them to bind his thigh and his

151

side just below his ribs.

Should have done this sooner, to prevent blood loss.

He pulled on the jacket and sat back and listened carefully but heard nothing dangerous. He closed his eyes, knowing he should rest but knowing also that it would be a mistake to fall asleep.

Safeguard the organism. Allow time for recovery. But don't sleep. Ten minutes, no more. Seventy miles to go.

★ ★ ★

The screech of the back door of the Transit being hauled open startled Dr Grace out of a moment of exhausted sleep. Elliot Pryce stared in at her, his face threatening. A group of men clustered behind him.

'Anything?'

'No, sir.'

'I have eleven people with me, hired at great expense. They need photographs of Michael Bannerman.'

'I have photocopies . . . '

'Well, dish them out, for fuck's sake, you stupid bloody woman!'

'I resent being spoken to like . . . '

'Bloody *do* it! Where have you searched so far?'

'I'm not sure. We've no maps or anything . . . '

Pryce snatched the handful of photocopies and handed them to one of the men. 'Where's this damned curry house, Doctor? What's it called?'

'It's not far away. The Taj Mahal in George Street.'

'Get that? He's armed: flick knife and cosh. Don't take chances. But I want him undamaged.'

The cluster of men dispersed. Pryce climbed into the van and pulled the door shut.

'Now tell me every last bloody thing you know about Bannerman's present condition, Doctor, just in case we decide to get rid of you at short notice. Which is probably what the Executive will decide, and I certainly won't be defending you.'

★ ★ ★

Marianne made a third cup of coffee and walked around Bannerman's flat, looking at the bookcase and into drawers and the wardrobe. A double row of wildly-assorted paperbacks, everything from Sherlock Holmes to sea angling techniques. A small selection of shirts and pants and socks. A raincoat and a pair of cords and a tweed jacket. A file wallet containing various National Savings certificates and a PEP and an ISA and bank statements indicating that he was not short of cash and that he was in receipt of a monthly payment which suggested an annual salary of about £35,000. His outgoings were a long way short of his income. Dr Grace had told her that Bannerman was still on the Spire Matte Interco payroll, although he was not aware of that. He thought his insurance and the fake award for damages had been invested on his behalf.

It was a rather sad little collection of personal belongings for a man in his middle thirties. No photographs, no personal letters. No friends, no wife, no children. No memories of good times. A man pathetically short of a life.

Where are you, Mike? Are you all right? Come home and let me take care of you.

★   ★   ★

'Coltard for Pryce. Over.'

Elliot Pryce snatched up the radio. 'Pryce. Over.'

'We have him. Sound asleep under a tree in a park, not far from you. He's in a state: filthy dirty, no shirt, bandages on his leg and round his middle, scratches on his face and hands.

154

He's holding a bloody great knife. We haven't disturbed him yet.'

Pryce checked his watch. It was a little after five in the morning.

'Can you get him out of there unobtrusively?'

'We'll need that Transit.'

'Tell me where you are.'

★   ★   ★

Bannerman woke slowly when he felt the hands on his arms and looked into the strangers' faces. His overriding impression was of cold and discomfort and exhaustion. He saw them take a knife out of his hand and fold it shut.

'No trouble, now, Mr Bannerman. We have a van here. It's just a short walk along the path and through the gate, then before you know it you'll be all nice and comfortable and eating your breakfast. Up you get, now.'

'What's happening? I mean, I don't know . . . '

'Someone will tell you all about it in due course, Mr Bannerman. Up you get, now. That's a good lad. Well done. It's this way. Not far.'

He tried to shake off the hard hands but they just gripped even more tightly. They took

155

him along a path and through a gate and pushed him into the back of a van where Dr Grace sat on a small seat looking very pale and tired. Beside her was a skinny middle-aged man with thinning hair and a sour expression. Bodies crowded in around him and the driver started the engine and the van moved off.

'You can let go now,' he said, very reasonably. 'I'm not going to do anything. You can let go.'

But they kept a tight grip on him. One of them even had an arm round his neck, which was offensive and made him angry, but when he struggled the arm tightened and he found it difficult to breathe.

He saw Dr Grace prepare a syringe and felt the sleeve of his jacket being pushed up his arm.

'I don't need that,' he said. 'I don't need anything like that. All you have to do is explain what's happening. I'm not violent.'

He watched the needle go into the vein and saw her bony thumb depress the plunger. 3 cc. No doubt one of the conventional quick-acting sedatives. Yes. Fuzziness round the periphery of the vision then the hollow feeling. Goodbye, world. Bastards . . .

★　★　★

At the Institute, Elliot Pryce watched the attendants strip Bannerman's inert body. First the watch, then the shoes and socks, then the filthy jacket and trousers and the white cotton pants, leaving him with bandages round his left thigh and chest. When the bandages were removed there were no wounds, only extensive scar tissue.

Pryce glanced through Bannerman's wallet then picked up the cosh and the flick knife in turn and examined them.

'Why did he bandage himself?'

'Because he was reliving what happened to him in Africa,' Dr Grace said. 'That's why he ran away and hid in the park. He thought it was all happening again. It was all so real to him that he thought the wounds were new and he applied first aid to himself.'

'So?'

I have to get a grip on this, Dr Grace thought. *I have to regain control.*

'This is what we wanted, Mr Pryce. It's all coming back to him. Something that has happened in the past few days has opened up a pathway in his mind. It may have been meeting his father: that must have been pretty traumatic and there would have to be an effect, a consequence. All we can do is let him run with it. Under skilled supervision, of course.'

'All right. But here, not outside. Twenty-four-hour surveillance.'

'I'm not sure about that . . . '

'I am. Do it my way or don't do it at all.'

'Mr Pryce . . . '

'Don't fucking argue! You're not in charge of him now — I am. You do what I say.'

★   ★   ★

One of the conventional sedatives, Banner-man thought, staring at the ceiling. Out like a light for twelve hours. Now I'm back in the bloody Institute and they're not going to let me out in the foreseeable future — if ever.

He closed his eyes and went into his mind and searched around.

Things seem to be a bit better ordered than they used to be. The episode in the curry house and later in the park, that was part of what happened in Africa. But I don't remember being in Africa. I know I was there but I don't remember it. But I do remember some of the things that happened there. It's a mess.

A young man in a white uniform entered carrying a tray and sat on the side of the bed.

'Supper time, mate.' He filled a spoon and pressed it against Bannerman's lips. 'Open up. Minced beef and potatoes and carrots.'

Christ, I'm belted in. I'm under restraint.

He opened his mouth and ate, the tears running down his face.

★　★　★

'What do you want us to do, Doctor?'

'Stay there for the time being, Liz. We don't know what will happen next. Bannerman may be able to return to the community and if that happens it would be best if he went back to his own home. Is Marianne there?'

'She's downstairs. Very unhappy. I think she got a bit too close to Bannerman.'

'That may have its value.'

'I think we're talking about a genuine human emotion, Doctor. Not something to be abused.'

'She's being paid to do a job, Liz. Remind her of that. Emotions don't come into it.'

'They do if you do your job properly.'

'Don't you start! There are too many bloody people telling me how to do my job!'

She's losing it, Liz thought. *She's under pressure from Elliot Pryce and it's all going pear-shaped and she's not used to dealing with problems like that. She prefers to work with the subject at the other side of a sheet of glass.*

She went downstairs and let herself into

Bannerman's flat. Marianne was stretched out on the couch reading an Agatha Christie.

'I've just spoken to Dr Grace and I've to remind you to keep your emotions about Bannerman under control.'

'They're under control. Did she say when he's coming home?'

'No.'

'So what am I supposed to do?'

'Hold on here in case they release him.' Liz read Marianne's expression. 'How close did you get? I don't mean the sex.'

'Very close.' Marianne's eyes flickered towards the cracks in the plaster where the cameras were hidden. 'Like I was instructed. If he's not coming home right away, let's get out of here and do some shopping. The larder's empty and I need to go to the cleaners and the chemist.'

They walked towards the row of shops opposite the park.

'OK,' Liz said, 'they're not listening now. How are things between you and Michael? Have you fallen for him?'

'Could be.'

'Dangerous.'

'I know. But you can't help these things. You just react. He's a good man who's been buggered about and it's not his fault. You can't help feeling for him.'

'Good sex?'

'Best I've ever had. And the most I've ever had, on a bonk-per-day basis.'

'Lucky bitch. You realize you may never see him again?'

'Don't say that.'

★ ★ ★

It was Dr Grace who released the webbing belts restraining him on the bed. He knew it was a symbolic gesture, calculated to make him sympathetic towards her, but Dr Leigh and two attendants were also in the room.

'Thank you.'

'I'm taking a chance, Michael . . . '

'No, you're not, and you know it.' He stretched his arms and legs but did not sit up. 'There was an incident. I got confused when a particularly emotive incident flooded my mind and I knocked over a couple of people, but I was running away, not attacking them. Then I fell asleep in a park. I had the knife in my hand because I was frightened. Self-defence. I wasn't violent.'

'Tell me what you remember.'

'I'd love a cup of coffee.'

One of the attendants left the room.

'Go on, Michael.'

He wiped his face with his hands and smelled curry. 'There's no beginning, no end. It starts with me escaping from somewhere. I have wounds to my leg and my side, my nose is broken and my eyebrow is split. Blood everywhere. I have to get under cover among some trees where I can't be seen by people in helicopters, then I have to get away from that place to a river and then to a border. I'm full of rage and I know I'm in pain but the pain isn't a problem. That's it.'

'What happened immediately before all this?' Dr Leigh asked.

'I don't know.'

'Think hard.'

'I've done that! It's not clear, not a memory. Just an impression.'

'An impression of what, Michael?' Dr Grace seemed particularly intent.

'Of being violent. Attacking people. A lot of people.'

'We've read your diary. You mention putting a bottle in your pocket. Tell me more about that.'

He looked at her blankly. 'What bottle?'

'You wrote about it in your diary while you were in St Andrews, Michael. A black man in a camouflage jacket shooting into a room at the hospital, Karen being killed, you being

162

hit. You put a bottle in your pocket. What was in the bottle?'

'You've lost me.'

The attendant entered carrying a mug. Bannerman sat up and took it and sipped. Decaffeinated, with milk and not enough sugar. He preferred his coffee black and strong and sweet. But it was hot and wet and he drank it gratefully. He could smell his own body odour.

'What kind of bottle was it Michael?'

'I don't remember a bottle.'

'Try to remember it. It's important. We'll ask about it again later. How do you feel now?'

'Sweaty, dirty, desperate for a shower and a meal.'

'You'll be under close supervision for a while, for your own safety, till we're satisfied you've got over this incident. We'll talk later about your trip to Orkney and your meeting with your father.'

They left. The attendant took the empty mug and watched impassively while Bannerman showered and dried himself and dressed in the T-shirt and cotton trousers and canvas slip-ons.

'You all right then, sir?'

'Fine, thank you.'

'I'll look in at regular intervals, sir. Your

dinner will be along shortly.'

'OK.'

There was a CCTV camera behind a wire grille high in one corner of the room, and another in the bathroom with its stainless steel sink and toilet and shower. Bannerman sat on the bed and wondered why he had lied to Dr Grace and Dr Leigh. He could remember the bottle very clearly. It was important, although he didn't know why. And it was clear that it was important to them.

More interesting was the fact that, despite the state of his mind, he knew not to reveal anything about it to them.

He could see, through the small barred window high on one wall, a grey sky and a small branch and a few leaves. Rather pathetic, after the vastness of the Orkney skies. He lay back on the bed and stared at the window.

I don't know who to trust. Cameras here and maybe in the flat. Men holding my arms and strangling me. Injections. Attendants. Questions. They want something from me, something to do with the bottle. Can I trust Marianne?

Yes. Surely. No one could be that compassionate — and passionate — and then betray me.

So now I have to get out of here. Legally or illegally. Whatever it takes.

Why?

He frowned and watched the leaves move in the wind.

I don't know.

8

The scratches on his face and hands had crusted. The feeling of bone-deep exhaustion was fading. His room was becoming more and more like a cell.

An attendant unlocked the door and entered and looked at him suspiciously then Dr Leigh followed, smiling. 'Hello, Mike. How are you feeling today?'

Bannerman swung his legs off the bed and sat up. 'Pissed off, Norman. Thoroughly pissed off. I resent being locked up just because I got scared by a memory and knocked over a waiter in a curry house. This is not the way to build trust between doctor and patient.'

'I know.' Dr Leigh dropped a net bag of fruit on the bedside cabinet and took the chair in the corner. The attendant stationed himself at the door with his hands behind his back. He was a burly man with a shaven head and a lot of muscle; he had the air of a someone who practised his lack of expression in the mirror and Bannerman had taken a strong dislike to him.

'What's the plan, Norman? What's going to happen?'

'First of all, Mike, our main intention is to protect you. It's always been like that. But we've given you a lot of freedom. We returned you to the community in the hope that you would gradually recover your memory and that worked, to a certain extent. You were quite happy for a couple of months in your flat. You met Marianne Shannon and formed a relationship and that was good. We let you go off on a trip trying to find something and you found your father. Great. But then you behaved erratically and we had to balance your recovery against the danger to other people. And that's where we are now. We have a responsibility to you but also a responsibility to the public and we have to juggle these responsibilities and we're at a stage where we're not quite sure what to do.'

'I don't feel dangerous. Anything but.'

Norman Leigh tried to cross his fat little legs but failed. 'There was the incident in Edinburgh, when you attacked two engineering students and put them both in hospital. You barged your way out of an Indian restaurant and were found in a distressed condition in a park with an open knife in your hand. You insist on carrying a knife and a cosh. You must understand why we feel it's

167

best that you're under observation at this time.'

Bannerman ripped open the net bag and took out an orange and began to peel it.

'So go on from there, Norman. I was really getting somewhere in the community, but I don't think I'm going to get anywhere in here. This place is repressive. All it does is to drive me back into myself.'

'Satisify us that you're not a danger to other people, Mike, and we'll be able to let you go back to your flat. Have you remembered anything new?'

'No.' Another lie. He obscured it behind the eating of the orange. 'There's no stimulus here, no chance to get the brain working. All I feel in here is resentment at being locked up.'

Silence. The attendant appeared to be exercising one arm against the other behind his back; the massive chest tensed and relaxed. Bannerman ate the last of the orange and chose a nectarine and bit into it; it was hard and tart and the taste reminded him of something but he couldn't be bothered trying to identify the memory.

'We're under pressure, Mike,' Dr Leigh said. 'The powers that be are pushing for results.'

'Why?'

'We have your best interests at heart, Mike, but it's a very expensive process. There's a Mr Pryce, one of the senior men, pretty well constantly on our backs demanding results. He's advocating a new line of treatment, a new way of helping you recover your memory. Stimulus. It's something that can only be done here at the Institute. We'll make a start this afternoon.'

'OK.'

'It won't necessarily be pleasant.'

★ ★ ★

'Can I visit him?'

'We're anxious that you do, but not yet,' Dr Grace said, watching Marianne on the screens; the young woman was sitting at the table in Bannerman's kitchen with a mug of coffee in front of her. 'We want to use the best possible moment. The best possible psychological moment. For the time being, we don't know when that will be. Are you still living in his flat?'

'Yes.' Marianne looked around. She had hoovered and dusted, washed the windows and spent two hours on the cooker and defrosted the fridge, washed the sheets and towels and his shirts and underwear and socks and his cords were at the cleaners. 'I've tidied up ready for him getting back. When will that be?'

'A few days, perhaps. We have to be sure of him. We have to be sure he's not going to be violent.'

'I don't think he'll respond well to being locked up. He was getting on so well when we went on our trip. It was difficult, but he was getting there. I could cope with him.'

'We'll see, Marianne.'

Marianne closed the connection and sipped the coffee. *I'm missing him. I'm not supposed to have feelings for a subject, but when you get to know a guy you can't help becoming sympathetic towards him. Unless he's some kind of bastard, and Mike isn't. I care what happens to him and I seem to be the only person who does. And the bed is empty with just me in it.*

* * *

This was a room he had never seen before, a featureless box with no window, empty except for one heavy armchair, a screen on one wall, a CCTV camera mounted high in a corner. There were four electrodes stuck to his chest and one on each temple; the leads ran across the stained carpet and vanished under the door. And this time there were two attendants

170

somewhere behind him. He could hear them breathing.

Dr Grace's voice came from a speaker. 'Relax, please, Michael, and watch the screen. We'll show you a succession of film clips and measure your physiological reaction, and you can tell us if your memory is stimulated or if anything looks familiar. It will all be quite painless, I promise. We can hear you. Ready?'

'Yes.' He felt nervous.

'Starting now.'

The screen came alive, in colour, the picture quality excellent. There was no sound. A sailing cruiser heeled before the wind with two people in orange oilskins in the cockpit; the image changed after five seconds to a long shot of a tractor towing a trailer across a field. An angler on a river bank; a woman mowing a lawn; an oil tanker on an endless ocean; a ballet dancer exercising; a man on a motorcycle herding cattle; a fairground; a path through a wood, sunlight slanting through the leaves; a playground full of children; fur-wrapped figures on a sledge drawn by a reindeer; a nuclear submarine at speed, displacing a massive amount of water; skydivers; the Boat Race . . .

Bannerman exhaled slowly and sank back into the chair. The images were on screen long enough for him to absorb and understand and then they changed, holding his interest. He sensed there was danger but felt he could handle it.

★   ★   ★

Elliot Pryce watched the screens and the readouts and the jiggling pens. Even he could see that Bannerman was showing no clear reaction to the images.

'Nothing.'

'It's very subtle, Mr Pryce,' Dr Grace said. 'It takes time to study the results.'

'Push it.'

'We have a carefully prepared pro- gramme . . . '

'Push it!'

★   ★   ★

The screen changed to black and white: Spitfires in formation then peeling off into a dive. Then colour again, a football match. Sydney Harbour Bridge with a power boat leaving a white wake; penguins waddling on snow; a Kalahari bushman shooting a tiny arrow from a tiny bow; jungle; a crowded ferry with minarets in the background; a wide river with three brown men paddling a dugout canoe; a waterfall

172

cascading down a cliff . . .

The screen went black.

'You reacted to one or two of the images, Michael, so we'll play them again and you can tell us what they mean to you.'

Yes, I was aware of something. I'm giving them information, revealing my secrets. They'll understand before I do and I don't want that. I want to retain some degee of control over my own mind. I need a place that isn't in the public domain.

Jungle. This time the film went on for about fifteen seconds before it changed to the three men paddling the dugout canoe. They had time to beach the canoe and climb out before the screen went black again. They had pudding-bowl haircuts and were completely naked and each carried several long spears.

'Well, Michael? What do you feel?'

He ran his fingers across his forehead and felt sweat. 'Heat. Humidity. I can smell decay and antiseptic. I can hear insects and voices.'

'Go on.'

'That's all.'

'No memories?'

'No. Just a reaction. It's obviously South America, the rain forest. Was I ever there?'

'That's what we're trying to find out, Michael. We're trying to find connections.

We're trying to find out who you are. Relax.
We'll move on.'

* * *

The smoke from Elliot Pryce's cigarette was
drifting into Dr Grace's face. She waved a
hand to create a draught but he ignored her.
He studied Michael Bannerman's face
intently on the screen.

'There's fuck-all happening, Doctor.'
Somehow, he managed to make 'Doctor'
sound ruder than the expletive. 'Let's get to
the point.'

'It's coming up, Mr Pryce. He has to be
relaxed first.'

'If he gets any more relaxed he'll fall asleep,
for Chrissake!'

* * *

Children skipping rope on a cobbled street;
surfers; a pipe band; a rank of Gurkhas stiffly
at attention; mountaineers with oxygen tanks;
a shark hanging from a crane on a dock; a
squad of black soldiers in camouflaged
uniforms, marching without precision, carrying AK47s; a burning single-storey building;
an F1 Grand Prix; two girls in mini skirts in a
busy street; a man with a bear on a chain . . .

The screen blanked out. 'We'll go back again, Michael.'

He knew before the film appeared what they would show. The black soldiers and the burning building. This time there was sound, unintelligible orders and a marching chant, the crackle of flames and distant shouting.

'Well?'

He shrugged. 'Nothing.'

'You reacted.'

He spread his hands. 'Sorry.'

There was a long silence, then Dr Grace's voice came back from the speaker. Her annoyance showed through her words.

'No problem, Michael. Keep watching.'

They'll do it again. Black soldiers, camouflaged uniforms, jungle, burning buildings. Be ready not to react. Anticipate. If I expect the image then I won't react.

How am I able to recognize an AK47? What do I know about Russian sub-machine guns?

They persisted for over an hour. They seemed to have a large supply of film of black men in various uniforms, of fighting, of atrocities, of dead black bodies, of burning buildings, of trucks full of angry or grinning black faces, refugees, white people in UN ambulances. To confuse them he deliberately forced a reaction to shots of horse racing and

Ayers Rock and the Great Wall of China and American Indians dancing.

The screen went black. 'That's all for now, Michael. Thank you.'

He could sense the defeat in her voice. 'Anything useful, Doctor?'

'That depends on you, Michael. Have we stimulated your memory?'

'I'm not sure. I'd prefer to be guided by your readings. It would help if you could let me have details of what I reacted to.'

'It's not that simple, Michael. You can go back to your room now, thank you. Or to the restaurant.'

* * *

'Well?' Elliot Pryce stubbed out one cigarette and lit another. By concentrating hard on the screens he was able to pretend he was not in the claustrophobic basement room. Almost. He wanted out. This was the longest he had managed down here and he was near breaking point.

Dr Grace glanced at Dr Leigh, seeking his help. 'We have a mass of material to study, Mr Pryce. Every reading and every change in Bannerman's expression will have to be correlated against the images. It will take time.'

176

'You don't have time, Doctor. You've used up all the time we're prepared to give you. Break the bastard now or get out of the way and let someone else take over.'

'Who?' Dr Angela Grace felt a terrible anger flood her body. She glared at Elliot Pryce, too angry to care what happened next. 'Who? Who's going to take over? Who knows more about Bannerman than I do? Who are you going to bring in to replace me? Some stupid bloody accountant like yourself?'

Pryce pointed a finger at her. 'You just blew it, Dr Grace.'

'Balls, Mr Pryce! Balls and more balls! You're out of your depth, shit-scared of the people above you, and you're panicking!'

Pryce glared at Norman Leigh. 'And what do you think, Doctor?'

'I think we should all calm down and accept that this may take a little longer than . . . '

'Jesus H. Christ!' Pryce strode across the room and flung the door open and they heard his rapid footsteps on the stairs.

'Claustrophobia,' Leigh said. 'I'm surprised he lasted that long.'

'Do you really want my job, Norman?' Her voice was shaky with emotion. 'It's no great prize. There are times I wish I'd become a GP somewhere in Devon or Yorkshire. Some-where quiet. Lundy Island, perhaps. Maybe it's not too late.'

★　★　★

Bannerman lay on his back on the bed in the darkness, the taste of toothpaste on his lips, and stared at the pale square of the window. Can they see me, in the dark, with their bloody camera? He closed his eyes and turned on his side.

Jungle. The Amazon. Amerindians. Black soldiers. Camouflaged uniforms. Russian guns. Burning buildings. Dead bodies, men and women and children, bloated and stinking in the heat. Blood spreading across the dusty ground. A black face at a window, sweating, the gun firing, the sound deafening. The machete flashing from left to right in front of him, the black head flying off. Blood spraying. Taking the gun and remembering to take the spare clips of ammunition and pushing the machete into his belt and running along the gap between the burning buildings and seeing them and stopping and knowing to take aim before firing. Watching them fall. Hearing the screaming. Smelling the smoke, smelling the burnt meat.

The sweat was dripping off his face on to

the pillow and his heart was thumping painfully and his breathing was rapid and noisy.

Go with it. Don't be frightened. Maybe later, if I write about it, it will all go away.

More of them. They were laughing, their eyes wide with excitement, their guns jerking as they fired at anything and everything, at buildings and jeeps and dead bodies. He reloaded and cut them down with a long burst and reloaded again and ran to the nearest bodies and took the spare clips and ran into the forest.

How did I know to lie to Dr Grace? What instinct is driving me to keep all this secret?

He wiped his face with the sheet.

How did I manage all this with bullet wounds in my thigh and my side? Where did I find the courage and determination and anger? I was never Action Man.

And how does South America come into all this? Am I just getting a lot of black people and jungles mixed up?

He broke the flow of images by turning on his back and then on his other side and wiped his face again. It seemed to have stopped. He felt the sweat on his chest go cold.

Another memory, but this time it was one to be savoured; he used it to steady his breathing and prevent the images of violence coming back. Marianne, laughing, leaning over him, her nipples touching his chest. Stroking her back, feeling the smooth skin. Feeling her weight settling on him, feeling her ease down on him until they were joined. The slow, gentle rise and fall. The silky skin of her breasts in his hands. The cool Orkney air coming in through the window. The cry of some kind of bird in the half-light.

He lay rigid. *I can't, not with that bloody camera watching me. They'll know what I'm doing. I want out of here. I've got to convince them I'm safe, harmless, that I can be released, that I can go back to Marianne. Either that or break out.*

★   ★   ★

This was a Doctor Angela Grace he had never seen before. She was abrupt, forceful, impatient. Doctor Leigh seemed cowed and nervous in her presence.

'We have to make progress, Michael,' she said briskly as she peeled the silicone paper off the sticky attachments for the electrodes. 'There's evidence that you're robust enough to cope with an accelerated programme, so that's what we'll be doing today.'

'What do you mean? More film of black men with guns?'

180

'Don't anticipate, Michael.' She attached the final electrode to his temple. 'Right, let's get started.'

'Can you tell me anything about the results from yesterday?'

'No. It might confuse you. We want you to react without any kind of influence.'

They started with a full ten minutes of safe images — sport, fashion, cars, people at work, sunsets and dawns and scenery. Then they hit him with an appalling image of bodies in a burnt-out building with black people standing by weeping, hands holding cloths over their mouths and noses; he could hear the weeping and cries of despair. That clip lasted noticeably longer than the rest. It was followed by an aerial shot from a helicopter flying along a beach, then Morris dancers, a regatta, Mongol horsemen, a whale sounding, people playing slot machines . . .

Bastards! Surely that shot of the bodies would provoke a reaction in anyone, not just me. I couldn't pretend I wasn't badly affected. What next? Back to the bloody Amazon?

Two minutes later the screen changed to show brown men in pudding-bowl haircuts hunting monkeys in the rain forest with blowpipes.

Now some more innocuous stuff and then

some more African atrocities. I bet you I'm right.

An hour later he reflected sourly that there seemed to be no shortage of ghastly images from Africa.

'We'll break there, Michael. Relax. You can go and have some lunch. Think about what you've seen and we'll ask you later about what you remember.'

The attendants disconnected the electrodes, leaving the sticky pads, and he went along the corridor to the dining room. They let him carry his own tray and make a choice from the servery but left him to eat alone. Dr Leigh joined him and tucked into his cottage pie with obvious appetite.

'Well, Norman? Have you succeeded in blowing my mind?'

'Relax, Mike. Don't blame us. We're under severe pressure to achieve a result. Elliot Pryce is an accountant and he see things very much in terms of figures and balances and totals and you are rather expensive. He's taken a dislike to Doctor Grace and threatened to fire her if she can't sort you out sometime in the very short term and that's a problem for her.'

Bannerman speared a piece of chicken and dipped it in the sauce. 'I know I was reacting to those horrible bloody images of atrocities in Africa, but anyone would.'

'Did they help you remember anything?'

Careful. This has to be done carefully. He put down his knife and fork and stared through the window at the grass and the trees, seeing the high chain-link fence with the razor wire along the top.

'I'm confused, Norman. The answer is yes, I suppose, but I don't want you thinking I'm getting a clear and coherent picuture. It's not like that. Confused images. They're becoming mixed up with the stuff you're showing me so I'm having trouble recognizing what's memory and what's film. I need time to think. I need to be able to relax and let the memories come back.'

'Good. That's good, Mike. Take all the time you need.'

'But not here. Not in the Institute. I find this place very stressful. I need to go home and relax and think about things.'

'I don't know about that.' Norman Leigh parked his knife and fork and drank his milk. 'All I can say is that I'll discuss this with Angela.'

'I don't need any more film, Norman. I think I'm suffering from information overload. My head's full of flying images and I need time to sort them out. But I think we may be close to a breakthrough.'

Give the little fart some encouragement. He needs it.

* * *

'Marianne, we need you to visit Bannerman and talk to him for a while and give us your considered opinion of his present condition.'

'All right. How is he?'

'Quite calm, quite relaxed. We're bombarding him with film clips, trying to stimulate his memory, and we think he's reached the stage where he should be allowed to react at his own pace, in familiar surroundings, with someone he knows and likes. You'll be quite safe.'

'When do you want me there?'

* * *

He'd been told Marianne would be visiting and had showered and shaved and dressed carefully, enjoying the simple excitement, the pleasure of anticipation. When the door opened and the attendant ushered her in he rose and held out his arms and they hugged tightly.

'Missed you.'

She looked up at him then turned to the attendant. 'Could we be alone, please?'

184

'I'll be outside, Miss.'

They sat on the bed, arms round each other. She studied his face.

'You look all right. Except for some scratches.'

'I'm fine. I had a memory come back and I got confused and ran away and hid in a park. No big deal.'

'When are you getting out?'

Bannerman stroked her hair. 'I think I'm close to that. They're worried in case I might be dangerous to people. Like you. I'm sure I'm not.'

'Would it help if I talked to them?'

'They're listening now. And watching.' He pointed to the camera.

'Bastards. How can you relax in a place like this?'

'I can't. I'm inhibited. I can't bear being watched. I need time to be alone and relaxed and think about things. They've been flashing images at me and some of them mean something and I need time to work at that.'

They were allowed to go along the corridor to the restaurant for tea and cakes, then Bannerman was returned to his room while Marianne was taken away to talk to the doctors. He was pacing up and down when the door opened and a stranger entered, the inevitable attendant behind him.

'I'm Elliot Pryce. I know who you are. Michael Bannerman, according to the records. You're causing me a lot of grief, Mr Bannerman.'

He was a tall man, thin, lantern-jawed, grey hair receding, grey eyes half-hidden under heavy eyebrows, the mouth a thin line, the prominent nose aggressive. His whole face seemed to be sneering. His suit had been made by a skilled tailor.

Bannerman shrugged. 'Sorry. Who are you?'

'I have various duties, Mr Bannerman, one of which is to oversee the work here at the Institute, and you are a serious drain on our resources.'

'So chuck me out. I'll go. Any time you like.'

'You don't sound very grateful for all the expert work that has been done on your behalf over the past nine months.' It was odd how everything he said seemed like some kind of accusation.

'I'm grateful, Mr Pryce, believe me. I'm very much aware that Doctor Grace and Doctor Leigh have put a lot of time into me and it's a credit to them that they've got me this far; but for them I'd probably be locked up somewhere, dribbling and talking rubbish. But I'm also pissed off. I'm tired of being locked up and I want out.'

'Sit.' Pryce indicated the bed.

Bannerman felt rage swelling up and fought to control it. 'I'm in a standing mood. I think I'll stand for the time being. You sit.' He pushed his face close to Pryce's. '*Sit!*'

Elliot Pryce sat down hurriedly on the bed. The attendant moved away from the door, arms swinging at his sides, ready to act.

'I don't take kindly to being ordered about like I was some kind of dog,' Bannerman growled. 'Don't talk to me like that again.'

Elliot Pryce raised a hand. 'Sorry. Cool it. Calm down.' He motioned to the attendant to retreat. 'Look, Dr Bannerman, you worked for the company in South America and Africa. You were given all the funds you needed. You sent home a lot of good results. But there was more, something you described in your reports but not in enough detail for it to be reproduced. Then there was a major incident at the hospital in Africa where you were based. You got mixed up in a civil war and all hell broke loose and you were lucky to get out alive. Your assistant was killed. According to the doctors, you were severely traumatized by these events and you've suffered from amnesia ever since.'

'What company?'

'Spire Matte Interco. You're still on the

payroll, Dr Bannerman. That's where your money comes from.'

Bannerman shook his head. 'I was in a car accident and there was an award and insurance money . . . '

'That's what you were told. There was no car accident. You were flown back into this country strapped into a stretcher and you were here in the Institute for a long time before being released into the community.'

Bannerman leant back against the wall and slid down until he was sitting on the floor. Elliot Pryce stared at him.

'What with your salary and your free accommodation here and in your flat and your treatment you're costing the company about four thousand pounds a week, Dr Bannerman. You owe us. You convinced us you'd found something of value, and we want it. It's very much a case of deliver or get the fuck out. We're running out of patience.'

★   ★   ★

Dr Grace and Dr Leigh watched the screen and listened to the dialogue. Marianne Shannon sat behind them. The tears ran down Dr Grace's cheeks.

'I can't believe he's doing this,' she whispered. 'Norman, he's killing that man.

Michael's mind won't be able to handle this. He'll implode. He'll turn into a bloody vegetable.'

'Mike's tougher than you think,' Marianne said. 'But that prick Pryce had better get out of there fast before Mike wipes the floor with him.'

★ ★ ★

Elliot Pryce stood up and moved to the door as if thankful to be closer to the attendant.

'I've arranged for you to go home, Dr Bannerman. Your girlfriend will take care of that. Your job is to remember everything about what you discovered and present that information to Dr Grace, as soon as possible, in detail. Five days. Do it. After that time we want the flat back and you're off the payroll and there will be no further treatment. If you come up with the goods we'll look after you and you won't be short of money. Think about it.'

★ ★ ★

'Surely it would be better if I knew the whole thing,' Marianne said.

Dr Leigh glanced across at his colleague. Dr Grace had managed to get control of her emotions but she was not yet in a state to deliver a concise and reasoned update on the subject.

'His memory is coming back, bit by bit,' he said. 'There's evidence that once this process starts it accelerates. There's also evidence that the mind protects itself by not remembering the bad things, at least not directly. Bannerman may remember events on the periphery of a crucial incident, but not the incident itself. And it's never a good thing to prompt the subject. You have to wait until his mind is ready to look at the core of the problem. That will be a bad time for him. Be ready for that, Marianne.'

'I'll try. Will he be violent?'

'No. That's not indicated.' He gave her a reassuring medical smile.

How should I know how he'll react when he discovers he killed forty-five people?

★   ★   ★

Marianne drove Bannerman's car home from the Institute. He seemed tense and said nothing during the journey, although he was clearly engrossed in everything he could see outside the car. She waited until they were in the flat and he had toured the rooms before saying: 'Good to be out of there? Good to be back?'

'Yes.' He nodded and smiled at her, a wide smile of great charm. 'Yes, it's good to be back. If you had any input regarding my release, thank you. I was stuck in that bloody place for months before they let me come here to live, and I'd hoped I would never have to go back. It's intensely depressing.'

He held out his arms and she moved into them and they clung to each other.

'You've lost weight, Mike. You're thinner.'

'You're still the same. Lovely. Sexy. Smooth to the touch. I kept thinking of you and getting a stiffy but I couldn't do anything about it because they were watching me on CCTV.'

'You mean, you got excited and . . . ?'

'And nothing, sadly. We have time to make up. If you don't object to making love with a loony.'

'You're not a loony, Mike.' *God, I hope I'm right.*

9

Bannerman woke at some unknown time in the darkness of the night, too hot, his mind whirling. He heard Marianne breathing quietly beside him and lay still.

She won't wake. We made love till there was nothing left in us then we both fell into an exhausted sleep.

He pushed the Downie aside and went silently and naked through to the kitchen and drank half a pint of cold milk then moved to the sitting room and opened the curtains. There was a pale light coming over the rooftops from the dawning sky. He walked up and down for a while, feeling his body cooling, trying to calm his mind, trying to lose the insistent flicker of images.

This is what I wanted, all those sticky nights in the jungle. To be cool. To stop sweating. To be comfortable. I used to dream of cool nights at home in Rousay, with the sea wind coming in through the window . . .

He stopped abruptly.

That wasn't a memory. That was . . . that was a conclusion based on memory. A deduction. An extrapolation. A . . .

Don't push it. Relax and let it come.

I'm remembering memories. No, I'm remembering remembering. I don't remember cool nights in Rousay, but I remember remembering cool nights in Rousay, and missing them. I can feel the emotions that came with remembering. Loneliness and hurt. The anguish of being abandoned by my mother. Hating my father. Being a very lonely small boy in a small house on a headland on an Orkney island, convinced that no one loved me, loving no one, hiding in my books, crying silently in hidden corners among the cold rocks. Anger, resentment, self-pity. Christ, I was a mess.

He started walking again, but the rapid succession of broken memories persisted, appearing and disappearing too quickly for him to recognize anything.

Calm down. Think of something boring. Walking along a beach, staring at my feet. One sandy step after another. On and on, endlessly. The beach stretching on forever.

He settled to the six steps between the kitchen door and the bookcase and closed his eyes and watched his bare feet on the sand and after a time the sand became rotting leaves and scuttling insects and he was following on the wrinkled heels of the old man. Ahead was the old man's son and behind them came the boy. They moved silently through the dim green of the forest, looking up into the canopy where the sun flickered through the leaves, watching for monkeys. Giant butterflies rose from the undergrowth. A small green snake hung motionless from a branch, beautifully camouflaged to look like a twig, yellow eyes watching him.

The old man turned and pointed to a fungus growing on a tree and said something and rubbed his scrotum, grinning. That word again. But this fungus looked different from the others.

Bannerman stopped and hacked a wedge off the fungus and put it in his specimen bag. The three Indians waited patiently. Their patience was bottomless.

Monkeys chattered somewhere ahead. They moved on, the Indians taking feathered darts from the skin pouches hanging on their chests and inserting them into the end of their blowpipes. The old man turned and motioned Bannerman to get behind a tree and stay there. He watched them creep forward, freeze, wait, continue, exchange signals, raise the pipes and blow the darts up into the canopy. Monkeys screamed and leapt from branch to branch; the hunters ran after them, Bannerman following, sweat streaming, his shirt stuck to his back. Then one monkey fell through the leaves and bounced on the soft ground, crying. Another followed. They twitched and screamed and bared their teeth and were killed quickly with sticks and the darts retrieved.

I don't mind the meat, Bannerman thought; *it's just that they look so bloody human when they're skinned, like children.*

He stopped pacing and looked out at the yellow sky.

So I was in South America. I can remember a specific day but I've no recollection of going there or coming back or what I was doing there. I can remember the heat and the sweat and the insects and the taste of monkey but nothing else. But I'm sure I was there. Before Africa or afterwards? Afterwards, if what Elliot Pryce said was true.

He winced, feeling a jolt of aversion. This was the first time he had allowed himself to think in detail of what the skinny man had said and he still wanted to postpone the shock of it, push it away, forget it. He had twice, earlier in the day, begun to consider the matter but had shied away from it. This was probably why his sleep was disturbed, why his brain was in an uproar. Perhaps facing the truth would allow him to rest.

He'd been brought back from Africa on a

stretcher and taken to the Institute. Therefore South America must have come first. There had been no car accident; everything that had happened to him, the physical injuries and the amnesia, had happened in Africa. So everything he'd been told had been lies. The car crash, his lack of identity, the enquiries, the insurance award, the damages, his income, all these were fake.

He went to the fridge and drank more of the milk. The vinyl flooring was cold under his bare feet. He returned to the sitting room and curled up on his side on the couch.

Spire Matte Interco. He'd read about the company in the *Telegraph*. A massive conglomerate: drugs, oil derivatives, property, transport, communications. *I worked for them. Presumably as a doctor. Doing what? Research, in South America and Africa. Research into what? Curare? Fungi? Monkeys as a source of protein?*

Civil war in Africa. That was no surprise. That was where the gunfire and camouflaged uniforms and blood came from. The atrocities. The hate and the rage.

That's where it all happened. That's what I have to remember. I've seen bits of it, but there's more. That's where the answer lies. That's what they want to know about.

He was cold now, huddled on the couch,

196

arms wrapped round his chest, trying to conserve warmth.

I should go back to bed and lie next to Marianne and get warm.

He was longer than the couch and felt increasingly uncomfortable but refused to move.

Four thousand pounds a week, Elliot Pryce said. Eight months, nearly nine. That's ... £140,000, roughly. Whatever I have in my mind that they want has to be important. Valuable. They wouldn't waste that kind of money on me if they didn't expect to make a profit. SMI is a company with a bad reputation for dumping staff when the economics demand it.

All those months, believing what Dr Grace and Dr Leigh told me about a car crash near Bristol. Bastards! It's hard to accept they were manipulating me to that extent. Maybe they weren't. Maybe they had some good medical or psychological reason for not letting me know the truth. Maybe they were genuinely trying to do their best for me. Maybe they were just acting under orders.

'Mike? Are you all right?' Marianne was standing in the doorway in her white towelling robe, indistinct in the grey light.

'I'm fine. I woke up too hot and came through for a drink and to cool down.' He sat up on the couch and covered his nakedness with his arms.

She sat beside him and put an arm round his shoulders.

'You're cold.'

'I like it.'

'Problems?'

'Remembering things. Trying to understand.'

She pulled off the robe and used it to cover both of them. Her skin was hot against his.

'How do you feel?'

'Puzzled. But in control.'

After a while she said: 'Shall I make a cuppa?'

'That would be good.'

'So who gets the robe?'

'My need is greater than thine. You're still warm.'

He watched her go naked to the kitchen without switching on the light. When she came back he raised the edge of the robe for her to slide under and cuddle up to him. They sipped their coffee.

'Good,' he said. 'Make me coffee for ever.'

'What do you mean?'

'I think I mean I want you around always.'

'All right.'

'You're beautiful. I suppose you always were, but since you got shot of your glasses and had your hair cut it's more obvious. I keep looking at you when you're not watching, marvelling that you're with me and not with someone else. When we were on our trip I could see other men admiring you and I got a kick out of that. I also got annoyed, sometimes.'

'I'm glad. I mean, I'm glad you like how I look.'

When they had drunk the coffee they went back to bed and lay with their arms round each other, trying to get warm, and Marianne quickly fell asleep. Bannerman stayed awake.

An attack on a hospital. Karen being killed. Me being wounded. That bit with the machete, cutting off the soldier's head, did I do that? Then grabbing the AK47 and the spare clips and shooting at the men in uniforms and running away. What's missing? What else could there be that I can't remember?

He tucked the Downie more closely around their shoulders and stroked Marianne's back gently, wanting to caress her breasts but afraid he would wake her.

What happened before the attack, and afterwards? The journey to the river and the border; eighty miles with bullet wounds in my leg and side, a broken nose and a split eyebrow. How did I manage that?

He slid gently out of Marianne's arms and turned on to his other side and stared into the darkness.

There has to be something in the middle. The succession of events isn't continuous. I was in the hospital and then I was at the far side of the compound, looking back at the hospital, seeing it burning, seeing the bodies of the children and the babies and the mothers. There's a bit missing.

He was half-asleep when he remembered the bottle.

A small plastic sample bottle with a screw cap, half-full of a pale liquid. A stick-on label. The number 37 written on the cap in black ink. Important enough for me to grab it while being shot at by black hands holding an AK47. I took care of the bottle before I checked on Karen, before I tried to avoid being killed.

What the hell was in the bottle? It had to be what Elliot Pryce was talking about. Important research. A major discovery. Something Spire Matte Interco wanted. Something valuable, which meant something that could be manufactured and sold in large quantities for immense profit.

And I've no bloody idea what it was.

* * *

Marianne used her mobile while Bannerman was in the shower and asked to be put through to Dr Grace.

'How is he, Marianne?'

'He's fine, really, Doctor. Happy to be back in the flat. Relaxed and optimistic. He says he's puzzled, trying to remember things. No indication of violence.'

There was a brief silence then Dr Grace said: 'I'll call him later today and encourage him to go on e-mailing us and keeping a diary. You could reinforce that. Ask him if he's doing it and remind him how cathartic it was.'

'OK.'

'Has he done anything odd?'

'He got up very early this morning and I found him curled up on the couch in the sitting room, naked, but he says he was hot and trying to cool off. It was hot, in bed. You must have seen all that on the tapes.'

'Yes. He sounded perfectly lucid. All right, Marianne, keep in touch.'

★　★　★

It was like being on holiday after the confines of the Institute. Marianne had days off and they went to Oxford Street and she shopped and helped him choose a new suit and shirt to replace the ones he had ruined in the park, then they had lunch and went to a movie. When they got home early in the evening Bannerman said: 'I'd suggest we eat out, if the idea didn't scare you. We could ask Liz along, if she's free.'

'Let's do that. But not a curry. Chinese.'

'Seems best.'

Marianne went upstairs and Bannerman unpacked his new shirt and spread it out across the back of the couch. As he collected the wrappings and the collar stiffeners he glanced into her open shoulder bag and was surprised to see a mobile phone. He'd had no idea she owned one. He had no memory of ever seeing her use it.

They walked the half-mile to a Chinese restaurant and over the meal, aware of the tension, he took great care not to say or do anything which might alarm them.

'You can relax,' he said between courses. 'I'm not going to do anything odd. I'm feeling very sane tonight. Boringly so. Sorry to be so dull.'

'That's all right, dear,' Liz said. 'We can't expect you to sparkle every time.'

'I haven't had a chance to apologize to both of you for that night. I'm sorry. Liz, has Marianne explained my problem?'

'Of course. Amnesia. I sometimes wish I

had a touch of that. There are a few men I'd like to erase from my memory for all time.'

'Rubbish,' Marianne said. 'You keep telling me about them. If you lost your memory of all the men you've slept with you'd have nothing to talk about.'

Liz shook her head vigorously at Bannerman. 'She makes me sound like some kind of slag, Mike. It's not like that.'

'I'm sure it's not, Liz. You're just a woman with a generous nature.'

It was a good evening, relaxed and light-hearted. They walked back to the flat with Bannerman in the middle, his arms round their shoulders, making them laugh. They stopped outside his door and Liz made a sad face.

'So you two vanish inside and do intimate and naughty things and I go upstairs to a lonely room and read my book and drink my cocoa.'

'I should be so lucky,' Marianne said. 'Mike starts work now. He does his e-mail and his diary. Well, he hasn't done it recently, actually, but he probably will tonight. Are you still supposed to be doing it, lover?'

'Yes, I should do a bit of that,' Bannerman said. 'But it won't take long. Do we have any cocoa? I have this sudden urge to drink cocoa and read a book.'

'Instead of making love? That's awful!' Liz looked genuinely offended.

'As well,' Bannerman said. 'Definitely as well. Delight upon delight.'

★ ★ ★

Dr Grace. A busy time, what with going to Orkney and finding my father and having a funny turn in an Indian restaurant and being locked up in the Institute and you torturing me with ghastly film of African atrocities and the visit from Elliot Pryce and learning the truth. Give me time. I'm putting together snatches of memory of South America and Africa, trying to make them into a coherent whole. I think I've reached the stage where I can recognize gaps in the memories, missing bits, sudden jumps in the continuity. I had a moment early this morning when I remembered remembering being in Orkney as a boy. What I mean is, I can remember thinking of my past life. I seem to have reached the stage where emotions are coming into the memories. Let me work on this. Bannerman.

He sent then went into his diary and rattled off a couple of pages then created a new document and began again, starting from the beginning, being ruthlessly honest, going back to erase anything that was less than absolutely definite.

Marianne appeared with a mug of cocoa. 'I'll get the bed warmed up. Will you be long?'

'A few minutes, no more.'

'It's midnight now.'

When he eventually saved to a floppy disk and deleted the original document and emptied the recycle bin it was almost three o'clock. He titled the floppy 'Spare copy start disk' and put it among the nine other disks then changed his mind and wandered around the flat looking for a safe hiding place.

Are they still watching me from hidden cameras or have I definitely dismissed that notion? Yes, of course I have. There's been no evidence that I'm under surveillance. Nevertheless . . .

* * *

'He's up to something, sir,' John Valance said, looking at Elliot Pryce and wondering why the skinny git seemed so tense. 'Last night he spent three hours working on a document then copied it and I think deleted the original and I think also emptied his recycle bin, then left the flat at 3.17 a.m. and we lost track of him till he came back at 3.36 a.m. There was no sign of the disk, but that's not conclusive.

The tail car was not on duty at that time and Marianne was asleep.'

'So you don't know where he went or what he did.'

'That's it, sir.'

'Useless bastards!'

'That's unfair!' Doctor Grace said. 'You can't expect . . . '

'Yes I can!' Pryce's fury crushed her reasoning. 'I expect anyone working for SMI to be competent, to do the job they're paid to do, to show a modicum of initiative! Another black mark, Dr Grace.'

'We'll make a search . . . '

'No, you bloody won't! That will be done by professionals. People who know what they're doing.'

She watched him storm out of the basement and listened to his footsteps on the concrete stairs and looked at Norman Leigh.

'You're silent and unobtrusive as always, Norman. It's quite sickening.'

'What do you think was on the disk?'

'Something that took him three hours to write. I'm wondering now if what we'll get from him in his diary will be the whole story or just what he wants us to know. I'm wondering if there are now two versions, one of them hidden. And I'm wondering what has prompted him to do this.'

Valance caught their attention. 'If I had access to his computer I could retrieve that document.'

'Even though it's deleted?'

'It's not deleted, even if he thinks it is. It's still there. He couldn't retrieve it, but I could.'

'His car is the obvious place to hide the disk,' Norman Leigh said.

Dr Grace picked up a phone and managed to intercept Elliot Pryce before he left the building.

'We may have a solution, Mr Pryce. Could you come back down, please.'

She replaced the phone before he could respond and made a gesture Norman Leigh had never seen her make in all the years he had loathed her.

* * *

Bannerman. Dr Leigh and I will see you on Wednesday, usual arrangement. Make sure your diary is up to date. We know Pryce spilled the beans and we're very worried that the shock may have been traumatic for you. We didn't want you learning all this suddenly. It's something you should have been allowed to work out for yourself slowly and gradually. Dr Grace.

Bannerman read the message while he ate his breakfast toast. Marianne had gone to work before he woke and, without her to set a standard, he felt slovenly sitting there in his robe, unshowered and unshaved.

Dr Grace. OK. Elliot Pryce was a bit of a shock, but I'm surviving. I have a lot of questions to ask you. Bannerman.

* * *

Marianne and Liz read the message on the screen in the office Dr Grace shared with Dr Leigh.

'What's he talking about?' Marianne asked.

Dr Grace shook her head, exaggerating her despair. 'Pryce went to Michael's room here and told him everything. Shock tactics, he called it. I could have strangled the perverted bastard. He could have set Michael back months, even traumatized him permanently.'

'He didn't say anything.'

'Last night,' Dr Leigh said, 'while you were asleep, Bannerman spent three hours writing something on his laptop then made a floppy copy and deleted the original. Then he left the flat just after three o'clock and returned nineteen minutes later and went to bed. We're assuming he hid the floppy somewhere.'

'So what's on it?'

'We're guessing. We suspect he's remembering more than he's told us. Can you make a stab at where he might have hidden it?'

'In his car?'

'We're taking care of that.'

Marianne shook her head. 'I can't think of anywhere else.'

★ ★ ★

John Valance sat in the back seat of the Primera with his briefcase in his lap and stared at the front door of the building where Bannerman lived. The thrill of being in a car with two men and a woman from a firm of security consultants had worn off during the two hours they had been parked under the trees. He wanted a coffee and a fag and a pee.

'There he is.'

They watched Bannerman come down the steps and turn right taking his car keys from the pocket of his tweed jacket. He stopped, turned, looked the other way. He walked along the pavement then came back.

'It's not there, dummy,' Coltard said. 'Believe your eyes. Your motor isn't there any more. We've turned it over and there's no computer disk in it and we've lost interest. Go call the police.'

They watched Bannerman go back up the

steps and vanish. Two minutes later they heard the bleeps as he tapped out a number then listened to him talking to the local police. Yes, sir, a car of that description has been found parked in Kew and is now in the police compound. Please come and identify it.

Bannerman appeared again and walked along the pavement, watching for a taxi. He vanished out of sight and Coltard turned to Valance.

'Off you go, mate. George, open the door for him.'

Valance watched George open Bannerman's door. It took less than fifteen seconds. They went inside and George fitted rubber wedges to stop the door being opened unexpectedly.

'On you go, chum. All the time you want.'

The laptop was sitting on the coffee table. Valance angled the lid for maximum readability and began to tap the keys. Ten minutes later he watched George relock the door and they went back out to the car and drove off.

'Where to, mate?'

'The Institute.'

★ ★ ★

Everything took twice or three times longer than seemed absolutely necessary. Bannerman sat in the hot building in the vehicle compound and drank bad coffee then took the phone book to the bench and searched for the number of Marianne's hospital. 'I have to speak to Sister Marianne Shannon, please.'

'Which ward?'

'Intensive therapy.'

'Hold on. No. sorry, I can't find a Sister Marianne Shannon.'

Silly bitch. 'The ward manager is Sister Douglas.'

'Sorry.'

'Well, put me through to Sister Elizabeth Parkinson in Orthopaedics.' Liz could pass on the message that he wouldn't be able to meet Marianne as they had arranged.

'We don't have a Sister Parkinson, sir. Are you sure you have the right hospital?'

'Thank you very much.' *You ignorant peasant. Of course I know which bloody hospital I've picked up Marianne several times at the front gates.*

He went back to the phone book and stared at the names and numbers and felt the chill of realization between his shoulder blades.

'Mr Bannerman?' The pretty coloured girl behind the counter held up a sheet of paper. 'Ready to go, Mr Bannerman.'

★ ★ ★

He got into the car and looked around. The mess of sunglasses and AA books and handbooks and service history and pens and chocolate wrappers in the door pockets had been disturbed; the floor mats had been awry and now they were straight; the screen wipes and spare fuses and old receipts and sweets in the glove compartment looked different. He got out and opened the tailgate; the dust looked different.

He drove back to the flat feeling tense and frightened and immediately opened the phone book and checked the numbers he had called earlier. Nothing had changed. Same hospital, same number. He called again and spoke to a brisk young man.

But Marianne and Liz were not there. They were not sisters at the hospital. So what they had told him was a lie. So all the intimacy with Marianne, all the whispered words of passion, all the caring and sharing and laughter and gentleness, all that had been false. Marianne was a spy, paid to entrap him, sleep with him, make him love her, make him tell her everything so she could report back to the Institute. There had never been CCTV cameras behind the cornices or microphones in the lampshades.

Everyone is lying to me. Dr Grace, Dr Leigh, Marianne, Liz. It looks as if the only person I can trust is Elliot Pryce. Out of the whole treacherous bunch he's the only one who's been honest with me.

He ran a hand across his forehead and felt the sweat.

I'm frightened. I'm panicking. I want to run away and hide. I'm surrounded by enemies, under threat. Those guys who found me in the park — they were a hard bunch. The attendants at the Institute. The Institute itself, that bloody room with its view of one sad little branch and a handful of leaves. The chain link fence round the grounds with razor wire along the top — why do they need that? Maybe there really are cameras watching me.

He went to the kitchen and checked the row of cup hooks screwed to the underside of one of the units. Yes; the spare key to Liz Parkinson's flat, the one Marianne had brought with her when she moved in with him. He ran upstairs and knocked on the door and waited then let himself in. It took ten minutes of searching but he found what he needed to know under a floorboard in a walk-in cupboard. It was difficult to be certain, but the cupboard was probably directly over one corner of his sitting room; he could actually see the narrow triangle of light coming from the room below. He was tempted to take the small grey unit and

213

smash it, but that would alert them to the fact that he knew he was under surveillance. There might be some advantage to pretending he was unaware.

He went round the flat, pulling open drawers, opening cupboards. There was a concertina file in a drawer under Liz Parkinson's underwear, everything neatly compartmentalized. She had been working for Spire Matte Interco for six years, on a very generous salary. She had claimed for all the meals the three of them had shared, right up to the Chinese of the previous evening.

The second file, underneath, turned out to be Marianne's, presumably hidden here so that he would not come across it. She had been with SMI for five years and appeared to be Liz's superior. Her contact lenses and hair styling and the sexy new clothes were entered as expenses.

Bannerman left everything as it had been and went back downstairs and made a cup of coffee. His hand trembled as he poured the milk and went to the couch and sat down. He left the key in his pocket, unwilling to be seen returning it to the hook in case someone guessed what he had been doing.

It was impossible to behave naturally knowing for certain that people somewhere were watching him.

10

The basement at the Institute was crowded. Too cramped and crowded for Elliot Pryce; he was finding it difficult to breathe. It was only by concentrating on the words on the screen that he was able to keep his panic under control. He finished reading Bannerman's secret document and looked round the circle of faces lit by the glow from the screens. Dr Grace and Dr Leigh, the two young women, the two technicians. Their close proximity was threatening.

'He's almost there,' he said. 'He's remembered a damn sight more than he told you. And he can see where the gaps are. He's building it up into a coherent whole, although he still hasn't remembered what we want.'

Dr Grace nodded. 'That describes the situation. But there has to be a reason for his trying to keep all this secret, and I've no doubt it was the shock of discovering everything he understood to be true was untrue. When you marched into his room here and told him everything you dumped him straight back into the state he was in when he recovered consciousness — no past,

215

no history, nothing to give him a firm place to stand. You've branded Dr Leigh and myself as liars, so now we've lost his trust. Now he has no one to communicate with. It's no use his remembering if he doesn't tell us.'

'We'll get it out of him,' Pryce said. 'I'm sure there are drugs . . . '

'Do you care at all if he lives or dies?'

Pryce looked at the young woman. Marianne. The screw. 'What?'

'Do you care at all if Bannerman's mind is ruined?'

'Yes, if it happens before we learn what we need to know. Afterwards, I don't give a fuck. And neither should you. Neither should any of you. You're not paid to care. You're paid to do what the company requires of you, which means what I require of you, and I require access to the prick's memory. Nothing else matters. Never forget that. If you forget what you're being paid to do I will send you down the tubes, taking your jobs and pensions with you, and you will have hell's own trouble finding anything better than stacking supermarket shelves for the rest of your lives.'

His intensity and the sheen of sweat on his face made the threat completely believable. No one spoke.

On one of the screens, Bannerman set a kettle to boil and opened a cupboard.

'You,' Pryce said, pointing at Marianne, 'stick to him like glue. Get him to talk. Let us know when he adds to his memoirs.' He turned to Dr Grace and Dr Leigh. 'You two can fart along as before. If you manage to learn anything, call me. If not, just shut up.' He patted John Valance on the shoulder. 'Nice work, John.'

Divide and rule.

He walked as slowly as he could to the door and pulled it open. The chance to exercise his power always left him feeling strong. He turned and looked back at them, knowing the act was theatrical but knowing also that it was effective.

'I want this matter resolved immediately. Fucking do it!'

★ ★ ★

I have to work on the assumption that they know everything about me, everything I've said and done while I've been in this flat. They must know I spent three hours writing last night then went out and hid the disk. Would they have someone outside all night? It seems unlikely, but I'll have to assume so, which means . . .

No! The car wasn't stolen — they took it so they could search it for the disk! Which

217

means *they* don't *know where the disk is,* which means there was no one watching.

He paced back and forth, the coffee forgotten.

I deleted the document and cleared the recycle bin, so that's all right. All safe. Now I have to calm down and work out what the hell I'm going to do about all this, find a way out, get free of them, because I'm damned sure that if I don't tell them what they want to know very soon they'll have me back in the Institute and God knows what they'll do to me then. Or what they'll do to my mind. They're ruthless. They don't give a damn about me. They could leave me beating my head against a padded wall for the rest of my life.

The phone rang. He hesitated before answering, then remembered he was showing on a screen somewhere.

'Hello?'

'Mike, I thought you were picking me up. Did you forget?'

'Shit, yes. Sorry, Marianne. My car was nicked and it took me ages to get it back from the police compound and I forgot. I'll come and get you.'

'It would be quicker if I just got a bus. There's one coming now. Must dash.'

He replaced the receiver; how easily the lies

218

came. He noticed the envelope tacked to the wall with his name on it. He hadn't needed to refer to it since . . . since meeting his father? He pulled it off and dropped it in the waste bin and felt a desperate need to talk to the old man.

Where was she when she called? The Institute? She's probably getting into a car right now. She won't risk being dropped at the door; she'll get out somewhere near the shops and walk from there.

There was a pub on a corner with a view of the junction and down the road leading to the flat. He ordered a whisky and soda and took a seat near the window. Twenty minutes later he saw Marianne and Liz get out of a Rover and start walking and felt a massive depression settling on him.

He had so much wanted to be wrong.

★   ★   ★

'Where were you?'

'We were out of milk and cheese and eggs and I wanted a paper and then I fancied a drink. I've been sitting in a quiet pub enjoying a whisky and doing the crossword. Couldn't get any answers.'

Marianne looked relieved. 'I thought you'd be here. I was surprised when you weren't. Is

219

it tomorrow your doctors are visiting?'

'Yes. God knows why. It never seems to do much good.' So far he hadn't managed to look her full in the eyes.

'Does this mean you'll be working on your diary?'

'I'll bring it up to date, yes. Though there's not much to say.'

'If you want to talk about it, I'll listen.'

He smiled at her anxious face. Playing out the lie seemed easier now that he knew for certain she had been dishonest with him. 'OK. Though I probably won't. It's boring.'

'It's important that you talk about it.'

'Why?'

'I don't know. To get it out of your system, I suppose. A trouble shared is a trouble halved and all that crap.'

You're so good at your job, Marianne. You really put everything into it; your emotions, your acting ability, your body . . .

He thought of the cameras and considered doing something outrageous, something to embarrass her, like pulling up her skirt and groping her, but found himself unable to do it.

She opened a shopper. 'I popped into a butcher and bought a steak pie. That OK?'

'Fine.'

220

Dad. I should have been in touch sooner, but these are troubled times. I seem to be at some kind of crisis point in getting my memory back and that's taking up all my attention. I want to return to Rousay. It would be so good to be there and absorb the silence and get to know you and Andie and relax. Please have the room ready for me in case I suddenly manage to get away. These days, when I have lunch, I keep thinking of the lunch we didn't have in the pub on Rousay and I feel I've missed out on something. My treat, soon as I get there. Come back to me. Mike.

It wasn't great literature, but the meaning was there. He sent and looked across at Marianne. She was lying on the couch watching television, her shapely legs drawn up under her, thighs showing, her head resting on her arm. She looked beautiful and desirable and it would be so easy to hate her, but he had been engrossed in her for so long that it was difficult to reverse his emotions completely. There were things she had done for him and with him which indicated a degree of caring . . .

'Doing your diary, Mike?'

'No. E-mailing my dad. I'll do the diary next.'

'I liked your dad. And Andrea. I liked their lifestyle. That's how I'd like to live some day. On an island, cut off, quiet and self-contained, no rush, no hassle. Open the door and look at the sea. That's my idea of getting it right.'

Is she being honest? Or is she just trying to place herself in my daydream? But I don't remember telling her about that little fantasy. It's new to me, barely formed, nothing definite.

When they went to bed he lay inert and she had to take the initiative. It was impossible to avoid becoming aroused, but he managed to lie back and let her mount him and achieved an orgasm without becoming emotionally involved. She collapsed beside him and got her breath back.

'It's better when we both do it, Mike.'

'Just the mood I'm in.'

'Tell me, next time, and we'll just go to sleep.'

She turned her back on him. He lay awake for a long time, staring into the darkness, making plans.

★   ★   ★

'It's Letitia. The subject left home at 9.34 a.m. carrying a holdall and drove north-east. We suspect he deliberately lost us in traffic. He shot the lights at a junction and nearly got sideswiped and we'd no way of keeping up with him. He was last seen on the A118 going towards Romford. We're cruising, but we're not optimistic. Sorry.'

'The stupid buggers are making excuses for themselves!' Elliot Pryce shouted. 'They just lost him!'

'They're very good at their job, sir,' Norman Leigh said. 'Lots of training courses and . . . '

'They blew it! We've lost him!'

★   ★   ★

Bannerman found a slot in a car-park on the front at Southend and went for a coffee then sought out a post office; he had to try three hotels before he found a tiny room under the slates. He opened the laptop and the file of papers and connected the printer. He went on to the net and arranged a new online bank account, giving his father's house on Rousay as his address, then worked for an hour, writing letters and printing them, filling in forms, addressing envelopes and stamping them. It was the first time he had looked in detail at the bundle of investments and compared them with the stock market prices in the *Telegraph* and he was startled by the total.

The bulk of all this must have been savings from before I lost my memory. They must have cashed in and reinvested so the dates wouldn't be a giveaway. At least they were honest. I seem to have been an enthusiastic saver. And I probably lived on my expenses and banked my salary while I was in South America and Africa.

He walked back to the post office and posted the letters then went into the nearest pub and ordered a pint and a bar meal.

Good. Getting organized. Clearing the feet, as it were. Getting rid of encumbrances. Financing myself. Mobilizing.

He had intended quitting the hotel room and returning to the flat when he had finished the paperwork but there was something about the anonymity and the silence and the freedom from surveillance which appealed to him and he stayed on. He bought a razor and pants and a shirt and socks then slept for an hour during the afternoon before going out again to spend an hour in a pub then wandered around until he found a seafood restaurant. When he left he went into a cinema and relaxed in the darkness then walked back to the hotel and went up to his room and connected and checked his mail.

Mike. Your room is ready. Redecorated, double bed in case you bring Marianne. The odd thing is, you've already given me everything I ever wanted. Hard to explain. Dad.

Bannerman read and reread the message, the tears running down his face.

Dad. See you soon. Mike.

There was a message from Dr Grace. He considered deleting it unread it then changed his mind and clicked.

Michael. I'm worried about you. Mr Pryce had no right to shock you like that by revealing your past. You weren't ready for it. Your mind is too fragile to be hit with that kind of information this early. We'll talk about it tomorrow. I've been trying to phone you all day but no reply. Where have you been? Dr Grace.

Piss off, thought Bannerman.

He went to bed early, tired, listening to the distant sound of voices and laughter and music in the street outside. The bed was cool and soft and fresh.

How long do I need? A week, probably. Do they have the power to intercept my mail? Would that matter? I've asked for everything to be done by credit transfer.

★　★　★

Elliot Pryce walked around Bannerman's flat. He stopped and glared at Marianne.

'Again.'

'His laptop and printer, the folder containing his private papers, these are gone, and a big holdall. The envelope on the wall that he used to remind himself of his name is in the waste bin. His shaving tackle and so on are still here and so are his clothes. He may have taken pants and socks; I can't be sure about that.'

'Why can't you be sure, damn it?'

'I never counted them!'

'Watch your lip, woman!' Pryce looked at Coltard, standing impassively near the door. 'Can't you do anything?'

'Yes, if you'll let me contact the police.'

'No. That's not on.' Pryce made an abrupt gesture. 'Get me Dr bloody Grace.'

Marianne used the phone and handed it to him. Pryce brought Doctor Grace up to date, giving her all the relevant information, then demanded: 'Where is he?'

'I don't know.'

'Work it out! Use your massive fucking intellect!'

'Possibly in hiding. Hiding from you, probably. You may have traumatized him by flooding him with information. Now he doesn't know who to trust and he's probably in hiding somewhere in self-defence, trying to understand, trying to get control of his mind. We told you not to . . . '

'You're repeating yourself. Where would he go?'

'Impossible to say. Somewhere else. Somewhere he can't be found.'

'How about Orkney? His father's place?'

'We could find him there. It's too obvious. He may just be in a hotel somewhere, not far away, wanting to be alone for a while. Maybe he wants to get drunk. Maybe he's walking into the sea at this very moment with his pockets full of stones.'

'Find him!' Pryce flung the phone at Marianne and pointed a finger at her. 'Find him!' The finger transferred to Coltard. 'Find him!'

His mobile rang and he took it from his pocket. 'Elliot Pryce.'

Marianne and Coltard watched the change in the thin face.

'Yes, sir. Yes. I've initiated a full-scale search. He's unstable, of course, which makes his actions difficult to predict, but we anticipate locating him very quickly and then we'll make sure he's secure. He'll be locked up once and for all. Yes, sir. I agree. It's time to take the gloves off. Whatever it takes. I'll keep you posted. Thank you.'

He closed the connection and glared at them and they could see the fear. 'I want him *now*! Fucking *do* it!'

★ ★ ★

Bannerman turned left with no interest in where the change in direction might lead. He had been driving aimlessly since he left the hotel in Southend after breakfast, keeping to the minor roads; at one stage he had seen a road sign pointing to Birmingham and later the sea had appeared suddenly in the distance. It was now early evening and he had no idea where he was. Terrington St John. Tilney High End. Tilney All Saints. He took another left. Terrington St Clement. He spotted a small hotel and parked at the front and found the bar and ordered a large whisky.

I think I'm approaching some kind of crisis.

A low, dark room, wooden benches and tables, wooden floor, old photographs on the wall.

A nightmare, probably. I'm shaky and agitated and weak. Marianne, I need you with me. I don't care that you're on the other side. I want you near me, ready to help, ready to bring me out of it and make me sane again, because *I think I'm going mad.*

He ordered a second whisky and asked about a bar supper and a room. The supper was no problem but there were no rooms left and it was most unlikely that he would find accommodation this late in the day during the season. Sorry, sir. He left an hour later and drove on into the dusk A few miles on, after two narrow misses with oncoming traffic and a jolting misjudgement at a corner, he braked and turned off on to an unsurfaced track and drove along it until he reached a gate and could go no further.

He sat with the engine and lights switched off, still gripping the steering wheel tightly, staring into the darkness. Then his head drooped and he closed his eyes; he could hear nothing but the sound of his own breathing and the creak of the cooling engine.

* * *

'There's unreliable word that the government forces will arrive at some time today, and we have no way of knowing how they will behave.' Sister Mary-Theresa was slightly under five feet high and thin as a twig and ran the hospital with unquestioned authority. 'We shall go on working as usual. However, it might be better if Dr Bannerman and Dr

Lipman were to leave and make their way to the capital. Or out of the country, since that seems the better option. We've all heard of the unfortunate occurrences in other places. President Okolo's forces do not appear to differentiate between friend and foe. Anyone is a target, especially anyone with a white face.'

'You have a white face, Sister,' Karen said.

'I have God protecting me, my dear.'

Bannerman raised a hand. 'Isn't God protecting me, Sister?'

'I'm sure he is, Michael, but there's no sense trying his patience. You and Karen are not actually members of the staff here, so your departure will not seriously affect the care we provide, despite all the assistance you have given us. I strongly recommend you leave immediately.'

Bannerman felt the sweat trickling down his face and the pain in his hands from gripping the steering wheel too tightly. It was as if all he had to do was hold on and listen and watch and see it happen. He could hear the voices so clearly.

'What do we do, Mike?' Karen's trust in him was a burden. She was a dedicated researcher, meticulous and careful, but not a good doctor. For Karen, medicine was something in test tubes and retorts and slides, not in people. And she was so desperately unattractive, with her big nose and flat chest and muscular legs. They had been sleeping together for three months and she had been hinting repeatedly at marriage and there was no way he could tell her their intimacy was based on availability and nothing else.

'I need a few more hours, Karen. I have to let this process continue till it's complete. If I stop it now the fungi will just start decomposing and the whole thing will collapse. I'm so close. I have to stay with it.'

'Can't you recreate back in the capital? Or in London or New York?'

'I don't see how. Not without another week trekking through the jungle looking for samples.'

'I can hear shooting. Listen.'

He went to the door and looked out at the dusty compound and recognized the fear in the faces of the queue of people on the veranda. The sound of small arms fire was coming from the south west.

'I think you should take off, Karen. Take my Land Rover. I'll catch up with you.'

'I'm not leaving without you, Mike.'

Get out, you stupid bitch! I can move faster on my own, without you to worry about. I'll steal a vehicle if I have to. I can travel across country on foot if I don't have to help you along. You'll hold me back.'

He took her face in his hands and kissed her. 'Please go, Karen. Without you, I'll only have to worry about myself.'

'I'm not leaving without you.'

* * *

The mixture in the retort was changing colour, from a dark brown to a clear golden colour. They watched, trying to contain their impatience. Karen had already gone to the room they shared and packed their bags and thrown them into the back of the Land Rover. She folded the filter paper neatly and dropped it into the funnel.

'Now, Mike?'

'Wait.'

They heard the sound of trucks approaching.

'It's them, Mike! We can't wait any longer.'

'OK.' He unclipped the retort and removed the stopper and poured the liquid carefully into the filter and watched the first clear drop appear and tremble and drop into the plastic sample bottle. Outside, the roar of engines, shouting, a crash as something was knocked over.

Karen went to the window. 'Five trucks.

Probably about fifty of them. Uniforms, so it's the government troops all right. It would be better if it were the rebels.'

'Don't let them see you. Keep away from the window.'

'They're spreading out, running. They're all armed. They're coming this way!'

A long burst of gunfire, then screams and crying.

'It's all right,' Karen whispered. 'He was firing into the air.' She left the window, unconsciously ducking, and returned to the bench. 'Can we go now?'

The plastic bottle was half-full. He capped it and wrote the number 37 on the lid. It was his thirty-seventh attempt at refining the combination.

Then the shooting began. The window imploded, sending shards of glass sparkling through the air. Karen collapsed backwards.

* * *

Bannerman raised his head and sat back and slowly located himself. In the car, somewhere in eastern England, at the end of a track, sweating profusely, shivering, feeling sick, still holding the steering wheel so tightly that his hands hurt. He released his grip with difficulty.

Success. What he had just seen slotted neatly into what he had already remembered.

Karen Lipman. Now I remember you and can honour you as you deserve. You loved me but I didn't love you and for that please forgive me. I was ready to but it never happened, even at our most passionate moments. You just happened to be the only suitable woman available at a time when I was engrossed in my research and needed release from the stress. I know I made you happy for three months and you did everything you could to make me happy and I'm grateful. If we'd both escaped I would probably have done the honourable thing and married you and after a while I'd have become blind to how unattractive you were and you'd have made a good home for me and we'd have had children and your family of doctors would have got me a high-paying job in the States and that would certainly have been better than what's happened to me.

He worked the muscles in his arms and shoulders and neck, trying to ease the tension.

You should have left when you had the chance, Karen. You shouldn't have stayed with me because you loved me.

You certainly didn't deserve to be left to

rot on a concrete floor with your brain exposed. *Pray God someone gave you a proper burial. Or that you were decently incinerated when the fire reached you.*

He found the door handle with difficulty and stepped out into the darkness and pulled off his jacket and tossed it back into the car. His shirt was wet with sweat and the cold struck through. He pulled it off and threw it away and stood there shivering, feeling weak and unsteady. The sky was clear, moonless, the stars bright. The silence was intense.

Am I going mad? Is this what it feels like? Weak, helpless, my mind out of control, lost somewhere, stripped to the waist, shivering, friendless, lonely, frightened.

He opened the back door and located his bag and used yesterday's dirty pants to wipe himself down then put on yesterday's shirt and the tweed jacket. When he switched on the engine and the lights he noted the petrol gauge and remembered filling up halfway through the afternoon. He reversed down the track to the road and stopped and got out and studied the sky, looking for the Pole Star.

There. So that's north. Now where do I want to go?

There was more to come. More memories. The gap between Karen being killed and the immense, glorious, electrifying satisfaction of blowing the bastards apart with the Kalashnikov. The bit between that and waking up in the Institute. But that wasn't going to happen tonight. He had learned to recognize the signs and this was not the time. He was empty.

Later.

★　★　★

'Well?'

Coltard opened a notebook. 'He booked in at a hotel in Southend yesterday and spent the night there and left after breakfast this morning. He did not have dinner in the hotel. No one noticed anything particularly odd about his behaviour. He spent most of the afternoon in his room then went out and came back late and wasn't seen again until breakfast. He paid his bill using a Visa card.'

'And?'

'There's no 'and', Mr Pryce. He left the hotel and vanished. We don't have the resources to find him. He could be anywhere.'

Elliot Pryce glanced at his mobile as if afraid of it then glared at Coltard. 'Find him!'

'If we could use the police . . . '

'No! We can't use the police. Too many explanations. You have to do it. All the people you need, all the money you need. Just find him and bring him back.'

You have to be the most frightened accountant I've ever seen, Coltard thought. Which I like. I'm enjoying seeing you shitting yourself Mr Pryce, because I do not like you.

'I'll put everyone on to it. This will cost you.'

'Just do it!'

★   ★   ★

'It's Marianne, Doctor. Any news?'

'Nothing. Obviously, he hasn't been in touch with you.'

'No. Nothing by e-mail?'

'No. Did you ever think . . . '

'What?'

'Did you ever see anything in him to suggest suicidal tendencies?'

'He was always very happy when he was with me,' Marianne said. 'Even when he was a bit down he never stopped being optimistic. I don't think suicide is an option. But you know him better than I do. What do you think?'

The silence lasted a good fifteen seconds then Dr Grace said: 'We have to take into consideration the fact that Elliot Pryce ruined everything. The effect on Bannerman must have been extreme. What we knew of his behaviour no longer applies.'

'So you think . . . '

'I don't know, Marianne. I just don't know.'

'Is there no news?'

'Coltard's with Pryce right now. They haven't seen fit to confide in me. I've already drafted my resignation but I haven't formalized it yet.'

'Don't do that yet, Doctor. Bannerman needs someone who cares about him.'

'Norman's with me. His pointy little ears pricked up just now when I mentioned the word resignation, but now he's looking worried. He doesn't really want the responsibility. I would genuinely love to dump him in it.'

'Hold on, Doctor. For Bannerman's sake.'

'Do you care that much, Marianne?'

'One takes an interest.'

11

He entered a village by a narrow lane and at the end of the houses found himself on a main road. The sky was lightening now. After a few miles there was a roundabout and a long straight and a sign indicating Boston. He switched off the lights and blinked repeatedly, knowing he should stop and rest, that he was a danger to other traffic. He found a roadside diner and parked among the lorries and used the dirty bathroom then ordered breakfast. Bacon and two eggs, sausages and black pudding, beans and tomatoes, toast and tea. He cleared his plate and sat back, feeling revitalized.

I can smell myself. I need a shave and a bath and a shampoo and clean linen. And twelve hours sleep.

But I'm not mad. At least, not right now. Now I'm very sane, a tired man who's had no sleep for nearly twenty-four hours, bung full of unhealthy food, yawning, smelly, wearing yesterday's shirt and pants and socks. You can't get much more normal than that.

He was able to buy batteries for the laptop in the filling station next door to the diner.

He drove on through Boston and turned east and followed narrow lanes across the flat land until he found a corner where he could park and open all the windows to let the breeze blow through the car. It was a day of cloudless blue, the sun already hot.

He worked for two hours on the laptop, describing everything he could remember from the dark hours of the night. It was fascinating how he could stop the action and look round the tiny room at the back of the hospital and see things he had not remembered. The fridge full of samples and beer; his boots and rucksack in the corner; Karen's strong brown legs under her shorts; her frizzy auburn hair tied back with a rubber band; feeling the shard of glass bouncing off his eyebrow and seeing the blood spout.

When he stopped typing it was because he knew what happened next — the shiny black face at the window, the deafening AK47, snatching the sample bottle and pushing it into his shirt pocket, finding Karen dead with her skull blown open, then . . .

Then nothing. A gap then the compound was littered with bodies. He had already remembered that bit. And after that was unknown territory.

He saved and closed the laptop and climbed stiffly out of the car and wandered around for a while, unsteady on his feet, completely exhausted.

The rest of it is going to come pretty soon. I can feel it. It's like a valve has been opened and my memory is trickling through into a reservoir and when that's full it will all flood out. I want to know but I'm scared of knowing. It's frightening, all this. I'm scared of learning about myself, I'm scared of what I may have done. I don't want to discover I'm some kind of monster.

★ ★ ★

A crisis meeting, Elliot Pryce had called it. Marianne and Liz were ushered into the conference room with the long table and matching chairs on the ground floor of the Institute. Dr Grace and Dr Leigh were already there, along with the security consultant, Coltard, and John Valance and Martin Brown. Pryce was at the head of the table and there were strangers at the other end, a man of about forty and a severely-dressed younger woman with a pad and pen in front of her.

'Sit.' Elliot Pryce looked around. 'This is a crisis meeting. A crisis meeting is aimed specifically at finding a solution to a particular problem. The problem is the whereabouts of Michael Bannerman. Mr Lethbridge is here to observe and report to the Executive. Now — where is Bannerman?'

No one spoke. Elliot Pryce looked aggressively from face to face.

'I want an answer! Dr Grace — eight months ago you were made responsible for Bannerman. He's still your responsibility. Where is he?'

'Running away from you, Mr Pryce.'

'That's not an answer! That tells us nothing. Where is he?'

'Running away. Hiding. Scared. He may be in a state of mental collapse after your incredibly stupid behaviour in revealing his past to him. I warned you . . . '

'Oh, shut up, you stupid woman! Dr Leigh — where is Bannerman?'

'I don't think we'll be able to ascertain that, sir, without asking for the help of the police. There are no indicators . . . '

'You!' Pryce stabbed a finger at John Valance. 'Can't you pinpoint him through his computer?'

'No. Sorry, sir.'

Pryce stared at Marianne. 'Hasn't he called you? You were screwing him; that has to mean something. He'd call you.' Coltard was monitoring Marianne's cell phone and the phone in the flat, without her knowledge, and

242

Bannerman had not called. The question was for the benefit of Lethbridge and ultimately the Executive; it was vital that everyone upstairs knew how hard he was driving these incompetents.

Marianne shook her head. 'Nothing.'

'So where has he gone? He must have talked to you about a special place, a secret place, somewhere he might run away to.'

'He found his father in Orkney, but I don't think he'd go there, not if he's hiding. It's too obvious. He never mentioned anywhere else.'

Two of Coltard's people had flown to Orkney the previous day and had already reported: Bannerman was not at his father's house. The operatives had found a bed and breakfast place nearby and were watching.

Elliot Pryce made an impatient gesture and turned to Coltard. 'No help from the hired hands, Mr Coltard. It looks as if it's up to you.'

'Call in the police. Give them his car number and description. I've already spoken to a contact in the police and if Bannerman were stopped for any reason and his car number queried I'd hear about it, though not necessarily immediately. It would be better to concoct a story and ask for official help.'

'We can't do that.' Pryce looked round the table, trying not to see the watchful face of

Lethbridge and his assistant's pen writing busily on the pad. 'Perhaps later. All right — get out! You're all bloody useless! Get out!'

He stared at his hands until the door closed then raised his eyes. Lethbridge and the woman spoke briefly in a whisper then rose and left without looking at him, and he hated Michael Bannerman with an intensity he had never felt in a long life of hating people.

★   ★   ★

Bannerman heard the voice and felt the hand pushing at his shoulder and it took a long time for him to struggle out of the darkness and open his eyes.

'Wake up, mate; come on, snap out of it. What's your name?'

Two policemen in shirtsleeves, bareheaded. They looked down into the car, their hands resting on their sticks, watching him suspiciously.

'What?'

'What's your name?

'Michael Bannerman.'

'Get out of the car, please, Mr Bannerman.' One of them held the door open and he eased himself out, stiffly, blinking, and looked at his watch. He must have been asleep for about six hours.

'You all right, sir?' The constable put his face close to Bannerman's and sniffed his breath.

Bannerman scrubbed his face with his hands, feeling the sweat and the stubble. They had cause to be suspicious.

'I'm all right, yes. I couldn't get a hotel last night so I kept driving then I got lost and I was knackered so I flaked out not long after it got light. God, I stink! Can you recommend a hotel somewhere?'

They checked his driving licence and took in the cash and cards then called in with the car number and appeared satisfied. The sight of the holdall and the laptop lying on the seat seemed to help.

'Where are you going, sir?'

'I'm touring, having a few days off, trying to sort out some problems with the book I'm writing. I find I think better when I'm on the move. I can listen to the characters better, somehow, and . . . '

'Your best chance of a hotel would be in Boston, sir. That way a couple of miles till you hit the A52, then go left four or five miles. And next time, don't leave valuables lying about where people can see them.'

'OK. Thank you. Sorry to be a nuisance.'

★ ★ ★

'Freiston Shore?' Pryce glared at Coltard. 'Am I supposed to know where that is?'

Coltard spread Landranger 131 across the desk and pointed. 'There. About five miles east of Boston, on the north-east shore of the Wash. A patrol car called in for a routine check on his car number at 12.46 this afternoon.'

'And?'

'That's all. Just a check. There are thousands of them every day. If you'd let me make an official enquiry . . . '

Pryce hesitated. Lethbridge and his assistant were sitting in a corner of the office Dr Grace shared with Dr Leigh, still watching and listening and taking notes.

'That was nearly two hours ago!'

'That's how long it takes, Mr Pryce. And there will be a charge, which will be on my invoice. Now, can I make this official?'

Pryce looked at Lethbridge and saw the grey eyes slide away. Lethbridge would take care not to become involved. Lethbridge was an experienced company man.

'Yes. Do that. Do it now. Have a good cover story.'

'I'll say that Bannerman is an outpatient who may have been given the wrong medication and we want to get in touch with him immediately. I'll say we know he's

touring in the Fens area.'
'Just get on with it.'

* * *

He had been rejected by suspicious recep-
tionists in two Boston hotels and had been
forced to buy a new shirt and tie, socks and
underwear, a pair of trousers and a packet of
razors then shave and change in the station
toilet to make himself look less like a wild
man. The third hotel found him a double
room. He stood under the shower for a long
time then dressed again and packed the
laptop and the folder of papers and went back
out.

* * *

'We have him,' Coltard reported. 'The local
police found his vehicle in a car-park in
Boston and he's booked into a hotel not far
away, but he's not in his room at the moment.
The police are treating this as a medical
emergency and watching the vehicle and
they'll be notified when he returns to the
hotel. We should have him before long. I think
we should have done this sooner, Mr Pryce.'
'What happens next?'
'I'll be notified. I have two operatives on

247

their way to Boston now to make contact with the police. The story is that Mr Bannerman is under medication for schizophrenia resulting from substance abuse and may react erratically due to faulty prescribing and that he should be handed over to my people so he can be brought back to the Institute for treatment. Dr Grace has confirmed this to the police.'

'This had better work, Mr Coltard.'

Piss off, you wank. Stop trying to sound like everything is someone else's fault when it's all your doing.

'Yes, sir.'

I hope Bannerman is worth all this effort, chum, because it's going to cost SMI a small fortune.

★ ★ ★

Bannerman woke as the train pulled into Nottingham. He found a taxi and asked for a hotel where he was sure of getting a room and was taken to a featureless grey block beside a busy main road. He gave his name as Norman Pryce and when he came back down he ate and went to the bar and sat in a corner drinking whisky and soda, waiting for some indication of crisis. After an hour or so he felt the first twitch in the muscles of his arms and

248

chest and saw the first indistinct image behind his eyes and went quickly up to his room and stripped and got into bed and switched off the light and gripped the bottom sheet tightly.

★ ★ ★

Food had been brought in and two coffee machines set up.

The personnel had polarized: Elliot Pryce alone at the head of the long table, the two doctors on one side, the two young women opposite, the two technicians nearby, Lethbridge and his assistant at the end, Coltard at a side table with an array of phones in front of him. Marianne Shannon and Liz Parkinson were still eating and whispering to each other. Dr Grace and Dr Leigh had conducted a barely-audible argument and were now ignoring each other. Pryce tapped his fingers on the table to indicate impatience with incompetent subordinates.

A phone rang and Coltard picked up and listened and replaced.

'Nothing. Bannerman has not returned to his car or his hotel. An appeal has gone out on local television and radio.'

'I didn't want that!' Pryce said.

'You asked for police assistance in a

medical emergency; this is what happens.'

'Shit! Was anything left in the car?'

'You'll have to authorize a search.'

'Do it!'

* * *

He dragged the door open and went out quickly, slipping on Karen's blood, crouching, and ran round to the back, hoping to escape into the trees, but there was a soldier at the corner, half-turned towards him, reloading his Kalashnikov, the purple lips wobbling, the yellow eyes frantic with excitement in the sweating face.

He felt something wet on his chest and knew without looking that the bottle was leaking.

The clip snapped home into the AK47 and the bolt rattled and the muzzle began to rise towards him. He ran the last two steps and kicked, aiming at the soldier's crotch but missing and hitting him high in the stomach with a terrible violence, forcing up under the ribs, probably killing him. As the camouflaged figure collapsed he grabbed the gun and turned and saw the youth who had killed Karen and cut him in half with a long burst.

Wrong! Overkill! But pleasing.

He looked down at the spreading damp-
ness on his shirt and felt tingling and then
fire.

Oh, Jesus Christ, it wasn't supposed to be
like this. This stuff has to be assessed in
dilute form under lab conditions on rats, not
flooded down my chest in concentrate. What
the hell's going to happen? It's burning me.

Suddenly, it was as if the lighting had
changed, as if the sun had gone out to be
replaced with arc lamps and spotlights which
illuminated perfectly whatever was important,
leaving everything irrelevant in shadow. Yes.
Like a film. Slow motion. I can move very
quickly but everything I look at is in slow
motion. Odd.

I'll need ammunition. These two dead
bastards have plenty. I'll take everything I
need from them. Spare AK47 as well, always
useful. Load and cock both weapons. And
take the machete as well.

He could hear distinctly everything that
was happening in the compound, the
shouting and the screaming and the gunfire,
and felt the anger becoming rage and walked
round the end of the building without looking
for cover and studied the slow-moving figures
in their uniforms and hated them. He could
see that there were twelve of them spraying
the main building with bullets and there

would be thirty rounds in the magazine of each of the AK47s. He began firing in short bursts, using both weapons, no more than three rounds for each target. They were moving so slowly it was easy to knock them down. Thirty-six rounds, eighteen from each gun. Twelve rounds left in each gun. Don't reload yet. No rush.

He could see the tiny figure of Sister Mary-Theresa lying in blood on the concrete steps, her matchstick legs exposed, and the rage blossomed in his mind and he went looking for more targets.

Three of them running out from behind a truck to his right, so slowly that he was able to pick them off with two shots each and then see that one of them was not dead and hit him in the chest with an extra round. Careless. Nine rounds in the left-hand weapon, eight in the right.

Eight — no, nine — of them were firing at him from the area around the kitchen. He watched the bullets kick up the dust at his feet and heard them whip past his head and felt one hit his right side and another go through his left thigh and walked towards them, firing single rounds because the magazines were almost empty. When they were all dead he reloaded and walked towards the main building, seeing the smoke beginning to roll out of the broken windows of the nurses' quarters. He stepped over Sister Mary-Theresa's body and climbed the steps and walked into the main ward.

Bannerman threw the covers aside and rubbed the scar below his ribs and felt the sweat.

I can stop it any time I want and start again. That's new. I'm getting control of it.

He stepped cautiously out of bed and went naked to the minibar and opened the half-bottle of champagne and drank from the neck. He felt shaky and weak, but not as weak as he might have expected.

Did I really do all that? Yes, I did. I know I did. The rage, the absence of pain, the slow motion effect, the weird lighting, that's how I felt at the time. And I know what I'm going to remember next and I don't want to remember.

He sat on the edge of the bed and drank more of the champagne and closed his eyes and waited.

The floor of the ward was awash with blood. He walked through it from one end to the other, killing men. He killed them as they hacked at the patients, as they laughed in ecstasy, as they drank the mineral water and ate the fruit, as they raped the women. At the far end he stepped out on to the veranda and began to reload and one of them appeared and smashed the butt of the AK47 into his face, breaking his nose, and he took the machete from his belt and decapitated him and finished reloading.

How many dead? He thought back. Thirty-nine. Karen had guessed at fifty, but that figure could not be trusted. He went looking for more.

One very young soldier being sick behind the pick-up; one bullet was all it took. Three of them in the dispensary, looking for alcohol; he killed them then chose a first aid pack from the shelves and pushed it inside his shirt. Six more trying to get away in his Land Rover; he aimed for the fuel tank and the vehicle exploded and he left them to burn. Two shooting at him from the trees; he aimed both weapons and blew them away.

Silence apart from the crackle of flames from the nurses' quarters and then there was the sound of more trucks approaching. He walked into the trees and waited, watching. Government troops. He let them park and get out and cluster, looking around, then started shooting but almost immediately ran out of ammunition. He considered going back for more clips but knew that was a bad idea and turned and set off for the river and the border.

After a few miles he stopped and applied wound dressings to his thigh and side and head. There was little he could do about his smashed nose.

The bottle in his pocket was empty.

It would be dark in an hour and forty minutes. He felt good, but it was logical to assume he would need rest. When the sun was split by the horizon he chose a place among the trees and sat down with the machete in his lap and closed his eyes.

★　★　★

That was what I was doing in the park that night, Bannerman thought. That was it precisely. I was reliving that night in the forest. The bit with the curry and the nan bread seems to have been wishful thinking, because I had nothing to eat that night in Africa, and I was ravenous.

He finished the champagne then showered in cool water and towelled himself dry and lay on the bed until his heart rate returned to normal. When he was ready he opened the laptop.

Maybe I will become a writer. I like writing. I like the loneliness of it and the singularity and the engrossment. It suits me. I like the idea of being totally alone, just me *and the words on the screen, the problems of communicating, the need for clarity, language as a precision tool rather than a blunt instrument.*

He rose again and prepared a whisky and soda with ice and sat down.

And you get to drink a lot.

He began to type.

★ ★ ★

Marianne woke at the sound of Coltard's dry, voice.

'It's now three o'clock in the morning, Mr Pryce. I think he's abandoned his car and won't be returning to his hotel. I think he's deliberately lost us, at least for the time being.'

She looked up the table to Elliot Pryce's pallid face and delighted in his stress.

'You promised me . . . '

'I didn't promise you anything.'

'You said . . . '

'No. I didn't.'

'Bastard!'

Nice one, Mike!

Liz woke and looked around vacantly, her hair a shambles. 'What's happening?'

'Shut up!' Elliot Pryce glared round the room. Dr Grace raised her head and stared at him without expression. Dr Leigh rose and went to the coffee machines. Lethbridge sat with his arms crossed at the end of the table, his eyes focused on one of the watercolours on the wall. His assistant slept on a row of chairs.

'Do you have anything further to contribute at this time, Mr Pryce?' It was the first time they had heard Lethbridge speak. His assistant woke immediately and sat up, blinking.

Mr Pryce. A few days ago it was Elliot. He drank my wine at £100 a bottle and smiled at me and shared confidences and suddenly I'm Mr Pryce. Bastard!

'Leave this with me, Gerry. I'll sort it out. It's clearly just a matter of time. If you want to shoot off ... .'

'I'll wait.'

'Can we go home now, please?' Liz asked.

'No, you fucking can't!'

★ ★ ★

The strange lighting was the first to go. There was a short period of confusion and then he was looking at an ordinary African dawn, the sky changing rapidly from pale yellow through golden to blue. Then everything around him seemed to speed up until synchronization was achieved. But the rage remained and there was still no pain from the wounds.

He jumped to his feet and started running, the machete in his hand, tireless, changing direction effortlessly, leaping over fallen trees, breathing easily.

Twenty-eight miles so far, estimated. Fifty-two more miles to the river.

He thought of Karen and occupied his mind by recreating the details of every time they had made love, from the first coy verbal hint through the foreplay and the passion to the required afterplay and the release of sleep. Then he remembered every shot, every impact, every falling body, counting them, pleased.

Forty-seven dead. Not quite enough to pay for your death, Karen. Not quite a fair exchange.

Noon, now. Blistering heat. Dehydration will become a problem. Find water.

He read the countryside and angled off towards an area of bright green in the dry brown and found water and drank until he could hold no more then walked for a mile or two then began to jog.

The wound in his leg was beginning to twinge a bit and he seemed to be breathing harder now.

* ★ *

Elliot Pryce woke from a confused doze to find Coltard gripping his shoulder.

'What?'

'A man answering Bannerman's description booked into a travel lodge in Nottingham last night using the name Norman Pryce.'

'Cheeky bastard!' Pryce looked at his watch. 9.15 a.m. 'Well, get on to it . . . '

'He left this morning just after half past seven, by taxi. He had dinner last night and drank a half bottle of champagne and two miniatures of whisky from the mini-bar and paid his bill in cash. We've found the taxi driver and this guy was dropped at the railway station. I have people on their way to St Pancras to intercept him. All this is assuming it is in fact Bannerman and that he's on his way to London. There's no guarantee, of course.'

'Nice one, Mr Coltard. Well done. It's always a pleasure to work with a professional. I want him brought here as soon as possible, and this time he will be locked up.'

Lethbridge and his assistant left silently. Pryce looked round the room at the grey faces. 'I don't need you now. Perhaps I never did. Get out. Have everything ready for Bannerman when he arrives.'

12

Bannerman left the rented car in a supermarket car-park and took a taxi to a junction a quarter of a mile from the flat and walked to the adjacent street. He found the passageway leading into the gardens and made his way round the perimeter, checking his sitting room window as he went, and entered his own building by the back door and went up the stairs silently and cautiously, half-expecting to find someone waiting for him.

He passed his flat door and went on up to the rooms Marianne had shared with Liz Parkinson and listened intently but could hear nothing. He knocked and waited but there was no response. He let himself in using Marianne's key, the one which had hung on a cup hook in his kitchen and which had been in his jacket pocket ever since he searched their flat for cameras, and locked the door behind him.

Coffee, but first a quick check. He glanced into Marianne's old bedroom then into Liz Parkinson's and froze. The curtains were closed, the room smelled of unwashed woman and the plump arm and tangled red-blonde hair on the pillow were unmistakable. He closed the door silently and swore. He had not expected Liz to be here at this time. He had anticipated someone watching for him getting off a train from Nottingham and had made the journey by rented car instead; he had assumed his flat would be under observation from the Ford Fiesta and had come through the gardens; but he had not expected to find Marianne's friend in bed this late in the morning.

He made coffee silently then took the mug and his holdall into Marianne's bedroom and closed the door and kept away from the window. The only way he could work was to sit on the bed with the laptop on the bedside cabinet. He collected his thoughts before switching on.

I've got it all, now. It has all come back to me, sometime between last night and this morning, quite gently and unobtrusively, no trauma, no breakdown, no collapse. It's a bit like loading the Encyclopaedia Britannica into the computer: everywhere I look there is a mass of information, too much for me to handle all at once. My whole life. But I can read all about it if I just look in the right place.

He thought of his mother. Blonde and

beautiful, laughing, careless, impatient. The hurt he and his father had felt when she left. *You were better off without her, Dad. Ultimately, so was I, but by then the damage had been done.*

Stepping out of the small plane on to the jungle airstrip, knocked back by the heat and the humidity. Meeting Xinu, the Indian interpreter and guide. Easing himself into the dugout canoe with its ludicrous outboard engine for the three-day trip upriver.

Seeing his father's face in the crowd at his graduation ceremony, recognizing the pride and hating it, making no effort to be pleasant. *I'm sorry, Dad. I'll make it up to you, somehow.*

Meeting Elliot Pryce in London on his return after a year in South America and taking an instinctive dislike to him.

'We've read your reports with interest, Dr Bannerman. Interesting, but inconclusive. Why do you think additional research in Africa would help?'

'There are various tribes in Africa doing the same thing, Mr Pryce. I need to compare their methods with what I've learned in South America. That way I hope to be able to isolate the specific chemical which creates the effect. At the moment I have something like ninety different compounds which may be

relevant, and it will take years to work through them all. By isolating the African compounds I should be able to test by comparison and eliminate a large proportion of them. It will save time and it may also lead us to a better synthesis.'

'Do they really just crush a lot of fungi and rub the juice into their bollocks and go fighting mad?'

'They use three specific fungi and they add a beer made by chewing some roots, but, yes, that's broadly what happens. They could apply the juice anywhere, but they regard the genitalia as the source of courage and manhood. It's said that some men drank the juice but they just went mad.'

'You're expensive, Doctor. How long will you need?'

'A year at the most. And I'm not expensive.'

Playing rugby on muddy pitches. Drinking in Deacon Brodie's and Scott's and along Rose Street. Making love in rooms all over Edinburgh. Having to cycle everywhere because he couldn't afford a car. Buying his clothes from charity shops. Working in the basement at Jenner's to pay his way. Trying to pretend he despised the money his father sent him every month, but always desperate to get it.

Getting a taxi from the airport into the capital, astonished by the chaotic mixture of squalid shanties and modern buildings. Buying a second-hand Land Rover before driving up-country. Sister Mary-Theresa showing him round the hospital.

'We have very little money, Dr Bannerman. We have aspirin and industrial strength disinfectant and a few drugs and plenty of TLC and we make up the rest as we go along. You're welcome to use the facilities for your research on the understanding that you pitch in with the ward work and the surgery.'

Bannerman listened to the subdued snoring from next door.

I'm ready. I don't have to wait for the memory now; I can summon it whenever I want. I don't even need the floppy with my first attempt at pulling it all together, the one I wandered about trying to hide and eventually slipped under a corner of the carpet in the front hall.

★ ★ ★

'He hasn't got off a train. Not yet anyway. We'll keep watching.'

Pryce glared at Coltard. 'You said . . . '

'No, I didn't. I said we'd watch in case. We're fairly sure he was in Nottingham and

264

we guessed he might be on his way back to London by train, but we'd no proof of that. He could have gone somewhere else, or rented a car or hitch-hiked. He could have gone to West Midlands airport and got on a plane. He could have gone to Edinburgh or Amsterdam or New York. All we know is that he hasn't so far got off a train from Nottingham at St Pancras.'

'Useless prick!'

★　★　★

So now I know. The effect of the compound begins to wear off after about twenty-four hours but it takes quite a while. The funny lighting goes first, then the feeling of operating at about ten times the speed of everything around me slows down. Then the rage goes. Then the anaesthetic effect. Finally the superhuman strength.

Christ but I'm tired!

How far to go to the river? I don't know. So there's another effect vanished, the ability to count, the ability to think back and calculate numbers of dead bodies, numbers of bullets used and remaining, number of miles travelled. And I'm dry and hungry, which I wasn't before, and I've had to tighten my belt a notch because I'm burning body fat for energy. *I must have lost at least a stone since I spilled that bloody stuff down my front.*

Stopping at the top of a low hill, looking around, gasping for breath, the exhaustion spreading through him like a cold fever, strength oozing away.

I could die here. My heart could just stop working, out of sheer exhaustion and overloading. Or I could go mad. The old brain is not working as it should. Fuzzy round the edges. Slow.

Seeing a village, smoke rising, small black figures, cattle, a pick-up truck. Walking down, not running now, staggering. Getting rid of the machete because it was a threat. The children hiding, watching him from behind the huts. Finding the man with the pick-up. Talking to him in French, making promises of big money.

Sitting in the truck, eyes closed, hurting badly, infinitely thankful that he had not tightened the cap on the bottle, that he'd lost it all.

Everything he had discovered had to be kept secret. The knowledge was too dangerous.

Even with his memory restored there was little he could identify of the time between blacking out in the pick-up and coming to six weeks later in the Institute.

I hope someone paid the guy with the truck.

It was as if the exhaustion he had felt then was contagious. He lay back on Marianne's bed and closed his eyes.

★ ★ ★

'Mike. Hello, Mike.'

He opened his eyes and looked up at Liz, big and soft in her robe, her hair untidy, her eyes puffy with sleep. He checked his watch: it was late in the afternoon.

'Hello, Liz.'

'You managed to find the one place in the country no one would think to look for you, but you snored.'

He sat up and stretched his neck. 'Are they looking for me?'

'Oh, yes. All over the place. Why did you come back here?'

'As you say, it's a good place to hide. And, as well, there's the matter of Marianne. I don't know what the score is, but I have to be sure.'

'She loves you, Mike. How do you feel about her?'

'That about describes it.'

'You know she — both of us — were being paid to keep an eye on you?'

'Of course. But I don't think she was acting

when she . . . There were times when she wasn't acting. Either that or she should take it up professionally.'

'She's downstairs. I'll bring her up.'

'Wait. Liz . . . '

'You can trust me, Mike. I was never your enemy. My job was the same as Marianne's — keep an eye on you and report frequently. For your own good. We were told you'd lost your memory and that we should get talking to you, stimulate you, help you remember. We know now there was a lot more to it, but we don't know the details. I'll never turn you in, Mike. And you can trust Marianne all the way.'

'OK. Thanks, Liz.'

'Your chances aren't good, Mike. You're being hunted by experts. If they don't get you today they'll get you tomorrow or next week or a year from now. They have unlimited resources and they won't give up.'

'I know.' He smiled at her. 'You know there are cameras in my flat . . . '

'Yes, I know. Sorry. I'll get her.'

He watched her leave then went to the bathroom and washed his face and combed his hair, wanting to look good for Marianne.

★ ★ ★

Liz let herself into Bannerman's flat and went to the bedroom and shook Marianne awake, conscious of the cameras.

'Come on. You can't sleep forever. I've made a meal.'

'Bog off.'

'Gin and tonic and ravioli and four cheese sauce. It's ready now. On your feet.'

'I need a shower.'

'Later. Pasta doesn't keep.'

*   *   *

Gerald Lethbridge and his assistant stood in the doorway looking at the small figure of Elliot Pryce at the end of the table.

'Let me know if anything relevant happens, Mr Pryce. We'll have to get back to report to the Executive.'

'Very good, Mr Lethbridge. Thank you.'

He watched them leave, hating them, then picked up the phone and rang down to the basement.

'Anything?'

'Parkinson has just wakened Shannon and they're going back upstairs for a meal.'

'Big fucking deal!' Pryce slammed down the phone then picked it up and slammed it down again and again and again.

Marianne followed Liz into the flat and rubbed her eyes with her hands. She had pulled on a T-shirt and jeans and felt sticky and unwashed.

'You could have let me sleep a while longer.'

'In there.'

'What?'

'Just bloody go.' Liz went into the kitchen and opened the fridge and wondered what she could cook for three hungry people.

* ★ ★

'You're not going to go daft on me, are you? You're not going to get violent?'

Bannerman shook his head. 'I've got my memory back. All of it. I'm normal again. Normal and boring. I hope I don't disappoint you.'

She sat beside him on the bed, suddenly wide awake, holding one of his hands in hers, intensely conscious of her unsatisfactory appearance. He looked good, calm, at peace, and she had never felt the way she did now about anyone.

'I have to tell you, I was employed to keep an eye on you and report back.'

'I know.'

'All the things we did, that was you and me. I couldn't fake that. That was real.'

'I knew, but I wanted to hear you say it. I've been missing you.'

They kissed shyly, almost like strangers, then clung to each other for a long time. When they went through to the kitchen they found Liz frying eggs and bacon, mushrooms and tomatoes. Marianne made toast. Bannerman made coffee.

'They're hunting you down, Mike,' Liz said. 'They won't stop till they've trapped you and locked you up. Pryce wants the doctors to use drugs on you. And we don't even know why.'

'It's money,' Bannerman said. 'Just money. What I have in my head is worth millions to Spire Matte Interco. Billions, for all I know. But it's the dirtiest money you can imagine.'

'That means they'll never give up,' Marianne said. 'Have you any idea how powerful these people are, Mike? They have all the money in the world and they can buy anyone they want and they are infinitely patient. They have contacts everywhere. You can't hide from them.'

'Twenty-four hours,' Bannerman said. 'After twenty-four hours you and I will be able to go anywhere we want and do anything we want. And if I do it carefully, Liz won't even lose her job. Did you really like Orkney, Marianne? Enough to live there?'

'I'd like one of those isolated little houses with a few acres of land near the sea. I never had a pony when I was young because we never had a place to keep one, but I'm still hoping. And I've always wanted a kitchen with a stone floor and a big dresser. No plastic work surfaces. That's important. Definitely no plastic. But . . .'

'Trust me.'

★ ★ ★

John Valance stared at the screen then snatched up a phone and called the conference room.

'It's Bannerman! He's in his flat!'

Elliot Pryce arrived first, followed immediately by Dr Grace and Dr Leigh. They watched Bannerman pour boiling water into a mug and stir then walk through to the sitting room.

'We've got him!' Pryce shouted. 'We've got the bastard! Call Coltard. Tell him where Bannerman is. Tell him I want the bastard tied down and delivered here immediately. All necessary force.'

Valance hit a memory button on a phone and started talking urgently. On the screen, Bannerman wandered around the sitting room and took a book from the bookcase and put it in his pocket.

'We've got him!' Pryce repeated, his pale face flushed with excitement. 'And he's going to pay for the trouble he's caused me! I'll make the bastard sweat!'

On the screen, Bannerman looked up at one of the cameras and smiled. 'Good morning, cocksuckers. Call me.'

Dr Grace glanced round the startled faces then picked up a phone and dialled. On the screen, Bannerman answered.

'Hello. Are you all there? How are you, Mr Pryce? How are you, Doctors? Rather relieved to see me, I should imagine, but don't fool yourselves. You haven't found me; I've found you.'

'Michael . . . '

'Shut up, Dr Grace. You're a disgrace to our profession. So are you, Dr Leigh. I'd prefer not to have to speak to you. It's you I want to talk to, Mr Pryce. Are you there?'

'I'm here, Mike.'

'Don't call me Mike, you unsavoury streak of piss. Dr Bannerman to you. I'm calling out of politeness to let you know that I am about to destroy you. I'm about to bring your ambitions and your authority and your position in SMI to an abrupt and cataclysmic close. How does that grab you, baby?'

Pryce glanced at the clock. 'Dr Bannerman, I think we should get together and . . . '

'Getting together with you is something that makes me feel thoroughly nauseous, Mr Pryce; you have the air of a man obsessed with women's dirty knickers. On the other hand, I would dearly love to get my hands round your skinny neck and squeeze till you go purple while kneeing you repeatedly in the balls. Your choice.'

Pryce glanced at the pad Valance was displaying: '20 minutes.'

'You seem upset, Dr Bannerman. What's happened? Is there something we can do for you?'

'What's happened is that my memory's come back, Mr Pryce. All of it. I know what you had me doing in South America and in Africa. I was trying to isolate whatever it is people of two different tribes on two different continents rub into their bollocks to make them go fighting mad, devoid of fear, able to think at ten times their normal speed, impervious to pain, untiring, not caring if they live or die. Even the immune system seems to be affected, and wounds seem to clot more effectively. If SMI could put a synthetic version of that drug on the market every screwball government in the world would be buying it by the truck-load. Maybe even the more civilized governments. Can you imagine the consequences? I've no doubt you can. I've no doubt you've had people doing very expensive projections to determine the potential sales.'

'Dr Bannerman . . . '

'Shut your face, you nasty little creep. I'm busy reviewing what you hoped was going to make you rich and powerful. The drug. In no time it would be on the market for sale to anyone able to pay for it. All those fanatics in the Middle East, all the African government troops and rebels, the terrorists and the suicide bombers, freedom fighters and police forces, warring factions in a hundred different locations around the world. Shit, before long you'd have football hooligans and neo-Nazis and hell's angels and white supremacists and New Age travellers and the UVF and IRA hard-liners and professional boxers and special forces and animal rights protesters and kids at pop festivals using the bloody stuff. You'd be able to name your price, Mr Pryce. You'd be chairman of Spire Matte Interco. I'm sure you dream of that on a regular basis.'

Pryce looked at the clock again. He had to keep Bannerman spouting off for a few more minutes. 'Dr Bannerman . . . '

'Shut up, Mr Pryce.'

Dr Grace pushed her face close to the telephone. 'Michael, we knew nothing of this! We'd no idea!'

'Yes, you did, Doctor. You knew enough. Maybe you didn't want to know any more. How long before your heavy mob arrives, Mr Pryce? Mr Coltard and his security consultants. I looked them up on the Internet. I've budgeted for fifteen minutes.'

Pryce swore silently. 'I can assure you, Dr Bannerman . . . '

'No, Mr Pryce, You can't assure me of anything. Let me clarify the situation for you. Just before I arrived here this morning I faxed every news agency, newspaper and television and radio station mentioned in the *Writers' and Artists' Yearbook*. It took me bloody ages to enter all their fax numbers. I told the story in plain and simple language. I named names — yours, the company's, the good doctors', the Institute's. I didn't name Mr Coltard, because I reckon he was just doing a job and will be eager to disassociate himself from you instead of chasing after me. And I didn't name myself. I should imagine there will be rather a lot of people with notebooks and microphones and cameras heading in your direction at this very moment. If you name me to them they'll find me and I'll be forced to give them lots of graphic details of what happens when you spill that drug all over yourself. I'll have to tell them about how you put a couple of cheap tarts into my bed in the hope of getting the information you wanted. I'll have to explain how I was hunted down by private thugs and how you planned to imprison me and drug me. Again, your choice.'

On the screen, Bannerman smiled up at the camera. 'Do you wish to comment, Mr Pryce, or are you mentally preparing your letter of resignation or just hoping SMI will find you a job in a fertilizer factory in East Germany? Nothing? Then I'll be off. Have a nice day.'

They watched him throw the phone over his shoulder and walk out of the flat. Valance took the phone from Pryce's trembling hand and placed it on the receiver. It rang immediately and he picked up and listened and held it out.

'It's a Veronica Terry. She says she's head of public relations and she's desperate to speak to you. She says their switchboard has gone mad.'

'I'm not here,' Elliot Pryce whispered. 'I'm

ill. Claustrophobia.' He ran out of the basement and up the stairs.

★ ★ ★

'Why Boston?' Marianne asked.

'I left my car there, and I have to return this one to Nottingham.'

'I should have left the mobile in the flat. It's the company's, not mine.'

'Throw the bloody thing out the window.'

'OK.' She wound down the window then paused. 'Shouldn't we call your dad first and let him know we're on our way?'

'Let's surprise him. Or we can call when we reach Orkney. Dump that thing.'

Marianne hurled the phone towards the grass verge. 'All gone. Mike, have I mentioned that I'd really like to have children?'

'Contain yourself, woman. You'll have to wait till we find a Little Chef.'

We do hope that you have enjoyed reading
this large print book.

Did you know that all of our titles
are available for purchase?

We publish a wide range of high quality
large print books including:
Romances, Mysteries, Classics
General Fiction
Non Fiction and Westerns

Special interest titles available in
large print are:
The Little Oxford Dictionary
Music Book
Song Book
Hymn Book
Service Book

Also available from us courtesy of Oxford
University Press:
Young Readers' Dictionary
(large print edition)
Young Readers' Thesaurus
(large print edition)

For further information or a free
brochure, please contact us at:
Ulverscroft Large Print Books Ltd.,
The Green, Bradgate Road, Anstey,
Leicester, LE7 7FU, England.
Tel: (00 44) 0116 236 4325
Fax: (00 44) 0116 234 0205

STRANGER IN THE PLACE

Anne Doughty

Elizabeth Stewart, a Belfast student and only daughter of hardline Protestant parents, sets out on a study visit to the remote west coast of Ireland. Delighted as she is by the beauty of her new surroundings and the small community which welcomes her, she soon discovers she has more to learn than the details of the old country way of life. She comes to reappraise so much that is slighted and dismissed by her family — not least in regard to herself. But it is her relationship with a much older, Catholic man, Patrick Delargy, which compels her to decide what kind of life she really wants.

PAINTED LADY

Delia Ellis

Miss Eleanor Needwood was about to be married to a most unsuitable suitor when Philip Markham came to her rescue. He arranged for Eleanor to be in London for the Season, a guest of his sister, who decided that everyone would benefit if Markham married Eleanor. And thus the rumour started. The surprised couple decided to play along with the mistaken impression until a scandal-free way to end the betrothal could be found. But when Eleanor agreed to pose for a daring artist, the result was far more scandalous than any broken engagement.

IF HE LIVED

Jon Stephen Fink

Lillian is a woman who feels too much. As a psychiatric nurse, she empathizes with her patients; as a mother, she mourns for her lost, runaway daughter. Now suddenly she has a new feeling, that her house, one of the oldest in the small Massachusetts town where she lives with her husband Freddy, has been invaded, violated by some past evil. And then Lillian sees the boy . . .

1	21	41	61	81		
	22	42	62	82		
	23	43	63	83	103	
		44	64	84	104	124